The Cowboy Way

BOOK 1 OF THE
MEN OF THE SPRAWLING A RANCH SERIES

BY

ANNA ALEXANDER

http://annaalexander.net/

HOUSE OF ROSENORN

The Cowboy Way

ISBN: 9780990595519
ALL RIGHTS RESERVED

The Cowboy Way Copyright © 2014 Anna Alexander
Print Edition

Edited by Gwen Hayes. Copy Edit by Eilis Flynn
Cover design by April Rickard with Dewpoint Studios
Cover photography by Jenn LeBlanc with Studio Smexy, Natalia Bratslavsky at
Dreamstime.com

Print book publication August 2014

An on the job accident leaves ranch owner Trey Armstrong with a dislocated shoulder and no recollection of the last few years of his life, including his marriage to the lovely Greta. His mind might not remember her but his body sure does, and despite his lack of memory, Trey finds himself eager to return to the homestead. With his ranch a success and a beautiful, understanding wife by his side, Trey comes to think he's been living the charmed life.

But not all is as it seems. Behind shy smiles and scorching kisses, Greta is hiding secrets that could destroy their rediscovered relationship. When the illusion of his perfect marriage begins to crumble, Trey realizes he can't live in oblivion forever and will have to remember his past in order to salvage his future.

Welcome to the Sprawling 'A' Ranch, where the men are as hot as the August sun.

DEDICATION

To my family, always.

ACKNOWLEDGEMENTS

You may have read or heard acknowledgements that begin with "this book would not be possible without…" and that is no less true for this book. Seriously, without the encouragement of Danielle Monsch, it might have taken years for The Cowboy Way to make it to the bookshelves. Thank you is not enough to express my gratitude for her mentorship, support and butt kicking. I also want to thank Carmen Cook, April Rickard, and Eilis Flynn for their encouragement and positive vibes for bringing Trey and Greta's story to life.

Thank you. Gracias. Grazie. Merci.

FIND ANNA ONLINE

Website
http://annaalexander.net/

Facebook
https://www.facebook.com/pages/Anna-
Alexander/282170065189471?ref=hl

Twitter
https://twitter.com/AnnaWriter

Newsletter
http://eepurl.com/Q0tsz

Chapter 1

"I'VE GONE OVER your CT scan several times, Trey. Besides the mild concussion and dislocated shoulder, there is nothing wrong with you."

Bullshit.

Trey struggled to keep the curse trapped behind his lips and shifted his body on the hospital bed's scratchy white cotton sheets. "Then why can't I remember?"

Dr. Grayson closed the folder in his hands. "It's common not to remember the details involving a head injury."

"What about the rest of it?" he bit out between teeth clenched against the rising panic.

"It'll come back in time. You have a good-sized goose egg on the back of your head, but there isn't any physical evidence of trauma to explain your loss of memory. The brain is a complex organ. Perhaps it decided it needed a break for a spell and is off on a little vacation and will return when it's rested. You've been working hard these last few years."

"Have I?" *Because I don't fucking* remember!

Trey closed his eyes and expelled a long, hot breath out his nose and bunched the bed sheet in his fists like the reins of an out of control stallion. The gold band around the third finger of his left hand felt like it was encircling his chest, squeezing the calm right out of him.

For the last two days he'd been in and out of consciousness. Two days of his life. Gone. When he had finally came to enough to be able to formulate a coherent sentence, the rapid-fire questions from the hospital staff had begun.

"What's your name?" a male voice had asked from his right.

"Trey, Trey Armstrong."

"What do you do for a job?"

"I have a ranch."

"What's your wife's name?"

"I don't have a wife."

The silence that followed had only lasted a few heartbeats, but the doc might as well have stuck a bullhorn right in his face and shouted, *Wrong, buck-o! You're married.*

In his mind the ranch he had grown up on was as crystal clear as high-def television, and the memory of his parents, who passed away a year apart, was still a bitter ache in his chest. But when it came to a wife or recalling his daily routine, his past was as vast and desolate as acre upon acre of rolling green alfalfa.

Good God, what else could he be forgetting, children? Hell, he hoped not. A family of his own had always been on his horizon, but the thought of having one now made his heart sink into his stomach. Children deserved to be coddled and cherished. He wanted to be the kind of dad whose kids looked to him as a hero, and there was nothing heroic about him now.

What type of asshole forgets his wife?

"And you're sure there isn't a bruise, or bleeding, or anything going on up there?" he asked again. A physical condition meant he could heal. With the right treatment he would be as good as new in just a few short weeks. Please, Lord, let this setback be as simple as a little swelling that needed a few white pills to set him to rights.

"I'm positive, Trey. The best thing for you is a little TLC."

Dr. Grayson checked the IV with a casual flip of his fingers, oblivious to the emotional tornado brewing in the hospital bed. Trey didn't like vague. He liked answers and action. The lack of a quick solution chapped his hide and made him want to shout a string of curses until the walls turned blue. He wasn't a patient man. At least, he didn't think he was.

"If it makes you feel better, come see me if you don't have some of your memory return in a week. Of course, if you start to have seizures or fainting spells, come in right away."

"Thanks, Doc. That makes me feel loads better," he muttered.

"We're going to keep your shoulder immobile overnight," the doc continued. "You'll be sore for a while, and you shouldn't do anything strenuous for the next few weeks. Keep off the horse and let your men do the ranching. Mark—do you remember Mark?"

Trey gave a tight nod. Yep, even the cynical grin of his best friend and foreman came readily to mind.

The doctor continued. "Good. As I was saying, Mark can take over the majority of the work for a while. Since you've been on IVs for a few days, I'm going to start you slow on food. I'll have some broth sent in. How does that sound?"

"Fine," he rasped. His throat felt like he swallowed a handful of rocks.

"Your wife's here. She's been sitting out in the waiting room. Would you like to see her?"

Dread and excitement filled his belly as his battered brain and heart engaged in a knockdown, drag out tug-of-war. Yes, he wanted to see her. For one thing, he hoped that seeing her would trigger his memory. Second, plain curiosity itched around his neck like an over-starched collar. Who had agreed to spend the rest of her life with him as a rancher's wife? It took a special type of woman to weather the storm of long nights during calving season and the stress of bringing a herd to market. She'd have to be strong of spirit and demand the same of him as well. Would she now hate him for not remembering her and his promise to love, honor, and cherish?

"Does she know about…?" He pointed to his head.

"Yes, she knows everything. I've told her to answer any questions you may have, but also to let you remember as much as you're able to on your own. It's going to be an adjustment for you both. She understands that."

She. He still didn't even know her name. Dr. Grayson looked at him through the thick lenses of his glasses, his eyes squinted in concern. "Would you like to see her?"

His ability to speak flew the coop. He nodded, muscles tensing as Dr. Grayson left the room. When the door reopened, his breath left his body in a harsh rush and he wondered if he was still knocked out cold and in la-la land.

Hell's bells and damnation.

Stunning. That was the only word that came to mind. Absolutely stunning. Long dark hair was pulled back into a low ponytail, revealing a soft chin and high cheekbones. Big brown eyes edged in mink-thick lashes looked at him nervously as her tongue swept over her full lips. His mouth went dry as he continued the perusal of the rest of her small and curvy shape. Soft and round, she was the perfect blend of girl next door and citified bad-girl that made a man want to strip away the innocent smile to expose the vixen beneath the cashmere sweater.

This was his wife? Again, what type of an ass would not remember being married to this beautiful woman? God, was he a lucky son of a bitch.

Apparently, his circulatory system was functioning just fine as desire stirred his blood, setting off another rush of guilt. How could he be getting a hard-on at a time like this? She was a stranger, a damn fine-looking stranger, but still, he knew nothing about her. What kind of a message would an erection send? *Hi, I don't remember you, but it would be great if you crawled into this bed naked.* Yeah, that would be a great first impression.

Her smile trembled at the corners. "Hello." Her voice was soft and sweet like warm butterscotch.

"Hi." A quick glance down assured him that his lengthening cock was covered properly. Thank God they unhooked him from the monitors, because otherwise they might have thought he was having an attack by the way his heart pounded behind his ribs.

Those dark eyes of hers raked over him as if she could assess his injuries by sight alone. From the top of his bruised head to the bottoms of his restless feet, her gaze sent the nerve endings tingling. He noticed the dark circles that marred her perfect skin, and he wished he hadn't been their cause.

"You don't remember me?" She drew the question out.

Trey took a good long look that went deeper than her outer beauty. He forced everything in his being to remember something, anything, about their life together. He pulled in a deep breath and detected her subtle vanilla scent, separate from the antiseptic smell of the hospital room. The perfume wasn't familiar, but it was comforting, soothing. When his head felt as if it was going to explode from the effort, he let out another harsh exhale.

He shook his head, defeated. "I'm sorry."

Her small shoulders slumped as she nodded, and her gaze fell to the floor. His arms ached to hold her, to give her comfort, which struck him as funny since he was the one lying there injured.

After a second, she lifted her gaze with a glimmer of resolution in her eyes. "My name is Greta. Margaret, actually, but everyone calls me Greta."

"Greta," he repeated and relaxed against the pillows. This was a start. She wasn't falling apart or running away. Yet. "How long have we been married?" The question sounded lame in his ears, but he figured he had to start somewhere.

"Six years." She took a step closer. Her head tilted in curiosity. "What do you remember? The ranch, the house?"

"Some of it. I remember the cattle, and the house I remember from when I was a kid. Does it still look the same?"

The corner of her lip lifted. "The inside is different. It's more modern."

Trey smiled back. "The house is pretty old. Three generations. I think."

"You're right."

Score one for him. "I remember Mark, and Ben, and Julio."

She nibbled on her full lip. "Julio doesn't work for us anymore."

"Really? Oh, well, I remember Roscoe too."

"He left about a year ago. Look, Trey, don't worry about remembering everything. You had quite a fall."

"I did? What happened?"

A frown touched her brow. "They didn't tell you?" He shook his head. "No one knows for sure. You were out on your horse Lucky. Do you remember him?" He shook his head again. What the hell had happened to his horse Chance, he wanted to ask, but she had already moved on. "Mark had been trying to reach you and you didn't answer your cell. The guys spread out to search and found you out on the far side of the property near the stream. You were on the ground, bleeding, unconscious.

Lucky was by your side. They called for the air ambulance and rushed you here." She blinked against the tears in her eyes but wasn't able to keep them from her voice. She stopped and took a deep breath while looking at the floor.

In a sick, twisted way her tears gave him comfort. She cared for him. He hated causing her pain, but her obvious distress over his welfare must mean that they were close and he wasn't alone.

"I'm sorry." She straightened her shoulders, visibly shaking the sadness away. "I haven't asked how you were. Do you need anything? Ice, water, another pillow?"

"Another pillow would be nice." He didn't need it, but he wanted an excuse to get a closer look at her.

Greta moved with swan-like grace to the closet and collected a pillow, then approached him with cautious steps. Her lips were pinched tight, and her gaze skittered away when their eyes met. Gentle hands helped him lift up as she carefully arranged the pillows. Her touch on his back and shoulder was more polite than amorous, but the heat of her hands seared him through the thin gown.

With her standing so close, he noticed her rich brown eyes were rimmed in red. Tears clung to the lashes, ready to spill over at a moment's notice. Seeing her pain and uncertainty pierced his chest. He wanted to reassure her that everything was just fine, but he couldn't. He was tempted to give in to tears himself, but squashed the urge like a bug under his boot. That wasn't the cowboy way. He would forge on however best he could and that was all there was to it.

Still, her sorrow called out to him, and before he realized it he latched onto her hand. They both gasped at the sudden movement, their gazes glued to where they touched. His hand looked so big and clumsy compared to her soft smooth one. Her little hand trusted him to look out for her, and now he didn't remember her. He had failed her.

"I'm sorry," he rasped.

Surprise lit her delicate features. "Why?"

"I don't remember you. I wish I did. I can't imagine how you must feel right now. Please know that the last thing I want to do is hurt you anymore, but I gotta know what I'm missing. Do—do we have kids?" he whispered the last part.

She gasped, then licked her lips. "No, we—uh, we don't have any children."

"I'm sorry I have to ask this now of all time, but I don't know what I'm forgetting, and I already feel like an ass for not remembering you. I'm so sorry. I just wish things were like they were before."

For a second, he thought he saw fear flare in her eyes before she squeezed his hand. "I understand, I really do, Trey. Don't worry about remembering. We'll manage somehow. I'm just glad you're okay. Well, that it wasn't worse, anyway." Her smile didn't quite reach her eyes. "We'll just take it one day at a time."

Trey nodded, not knowing what else to say. He knew what he wanted to do. Pull her close and kiss the tears from her eyes. But it was way too soon for anything husbandly like that.

A knock on the door preceded a nurse entering the room with a tray in her hands.

"Here is your broth, Mr. Armstrong." She set it on the table near his bed. "I'm sorry, Mrs. Armstrong, visiting hours have been over for a while, and Dr. Grayson wants him to rest."

She nodded. "I'll be just a minute."

Panic gripped him at the thought of her leaving. Greta was his only link to his past, and her presence was a great comfort. He clasped her hand tighter to keep her close for just a little longer.

"You're supposed to be released tomorrow. I'll come get you

in the afternoon, all right?" Her honeyed voice slid over his tight muscles, easing some of his tension.

"Okay." Reluctantly, he let her go with a slow slide of his palm. Had those little sparks of electricity always been in her touch?

Greta looked him in the eye. A thunderstorm rolled across her face as she bit the inside of her lip. Before he could ask her what she was thinking, she reached out and brushed a lock of hair from his forehead. The movement shot like wildfire through his body down to his toes. The fact that a simple touch shook him so deeply amazed him.

Her plump lower lip jutted out while her gaze focused on his mouth. His own lips parted in anticipation. Did he deserve a good-bye kiss? No, but he wasn't going to turn one down, either. He swayed toward her, caught between heaven and damnation.

The pad of her thumb brushed along his jaw. "Good night, Trey," she whispered.

"Good night, Greta." *My wife.*

Her lips curled up in a soft smile of promise and when she left, all of her warmth went with her. He heaved a deep sigh. Anticipation and excitement hummed in his vein. The electricity coursing through his body reminded him of how good it was to be alive.

What type of relationship did he have with the lovely Greta? He hoped the two of them were drunk with happiness, 'cause she certainly left him lightheaded. Settling back against the perfectly fluffed pillows, he started counting the minutes until he was released, and he could delve into the mystery that was Greta Armstrong.

Chapter 2

I T TOOK GRETA three tries before her shaking hand forced the car key into the lock. Her thoughts were so focused on Trey that she had completely forgotten about the unlock button on the fob. Once inside the SUV, she rested her head against the steering wheel and let the tears fall.

"He's okay. He's okay," she whispered into the plastic.

She hadn't believed Mark when he called her about Trey's accident. Her husband had been upright the last time she had seen him. He was stunned and in shock, much to her surprise, but at least he was still walking. What the hell had happened?

Seeing him in that bed, unconscious, weak, it had hit home just how much the man lying there was not the Trey she had married. She had married a man who wore a ready smile and a devilish spark in his eyes. Back then, he'd had enough confidence for ten men and never let anything keep him from what he wanted. That Trey she loved with her heart and soul, and she missed him. God, she missed him so much. The man she had seen hooked to monitors and tubes had been broken in both body and spirit. The guilt knowing that she was to blame tore her in two.

It was almost a blessing that he lost his memory, because if he remembered…

"Please, Lord, don't let him remember," she whispered over and over again.

The things she had said, the horrible things she said to him made her want to curl up in a ball as the tears fell faster. She didn't regret saying them. She just couldn't live through that experience again.

But now there was a chance she might not have to. A spark of her Trey was back. It was there in the light of curiosity in his eyes and the hint of the smile that had flitted nervously on his lips. The spark was small, but just enough to give her hope.

As long as he doesn't remember. He can't *remember.*

A knock on the window had her gasping as her hand flew to her throat. An orderly peered down at her through the glass.

"Are you all right, miss?" he asked.

Hysterical laughter bubbled to the surface. He had no clue just how far away from all right she was.

"Sure," she replied and brushed back the hair that stuck to her cheeks. "I'm just fine."

Chapter 3

NEVER HAD GOING home felt so good.

The thermometer on the dashboard read ninety-four degrees, but that didn't stop Trey from riding with the window rolled down. The brush of the hot, dry breeze on his skin was so much better than the frozen, recirculated air that had been pumped into his hospital room.

"Are you sure you don't mind me having the window down?" He asked again of his fellow passengers in the SUV.

Greta smiled from the driver's seat as she risked a quick glance in his direction. "No, you're fine."

He eyed her white-knuckled grip on the steering wheel and hoped to hell he wasn't the cause of her anxiety.

His memory hadn't returned. She said that it didn't matter, but he found that hard to believe. On some level she must be hurting because the man who once knew her on the most intimate of levels couldn't even remember something as simple as her middle name. Christ, what was her middle name?

Chalk that up on the list for the morning that had been filled with a bevy of what-the-hells. When he had gotten his first real look at his face that morning, he about fell on his ass in disbelief. Silver streaks blended in with the sun-tipped blond strands of his hair. Deep creases were carved around his mouth, and a permanent furrow etched his brow. He was only thirty-five, yet his dull blue eyes said he had lived a life filled with too much pain.

God, he hoped that once he was back in familiar territory, the memories would race back like a stampede.

He snuck another peek at Greta. She was strung tighter than a guitar string, and the compulsion to place a comforting hand on her knee rode him hard, but he wasn't certain if that maneuver would send them careening off the road, so he kept his hands to himself.

She sure did look pretty in a blue cotton blouse and hip-hugging jeans. Her hair fell in a chocolate waterfall over her shoulders held back by a black headband. The look was very wholesome, very rancher's wife, but the richness of her dark eyes and the pout of her lips hinted at a passion he ached to become reacquainted with. He wanted to replace the uncertainty in her gaze with drowsy desire, which was definitely not an appropriate response, given the situation. It was probably for the best they had an extra rider in the car.

Behind him Mark, his foreman, shifted his tall frame in his seat. Trey was grateful to see one familiar face, but his presence effectively put a damper on any quality time with his wife.

Mark was his brother from another mother. As kids, he and Trey had worked together on the ranch every weekend and all throughout summer. Mark had been right by his side after Trey's parents passed away soon after they had graduated high school. They had left the farm to a man-child who thought he had years to plan before that mantle of responsibility landed upon his scrawny shoulders. But together, he and Mark had worked the ranch until they knew the location of every tree, gopher hole, and rock formation. If his best friend was still working for him after all of these years, he must be doing something right.

Greta turned the SUV off the main road, and the earthy scent of dry hay became overpowered by the distinct and overwhelming aroma of cows. Many a city slicker turned tail and ran after that first inhale, but it was something Trey had grown up with. He drew in a deep breath and smiled. That bite of manure and dirt in his nose was so comforting, he sucked in another lungful with a long sigh.

Mark laughed. "I knew you'd remember the smell of cow shit. You're the only sick bastard I know who would wear it as cologne, if it were possible."

"I wouldn't go that far," he groused, mindful of the pretty lady seated to his left.

They passed under a wrought iron archway that read "Sprawling A Ranch." Split-wood rail fencing bordered the areas closest to the house, while barbed wire enclosed the rest of the rambling 15,000-acre spread.

"Welcome home, sweetie—Trey," Greta said.

He wished she didn't feel the need to curb her affection toward him. She probably thought he needed some space and time to readjust, which he could appreciate, but she was welcome to get into his space as much as she desired. If she wanted to call him "sweetie," by all means, yes ma'am. If she wanted to touch his arm, or give him a hug, even press her lips to his followed by those lush curves…yeah, he'd need to pull the reins in on those lecherous thoughts.

The two-story ranch house stood sentinel in the middle of rolling green grass the same as it had for the last eighty years. The paint was fresher, but the swing that had been there long before he was born still hung the front porch, swaying gently in the afternoon breeze.

Parked next to the garage was a huge Ford F-350 Super Duty

that made his jaw drop and a bit of drool collect at the corner of his mouth. Those babies had a 400-horsepower engine and were capable of over 24,000 pounds of hauling capacity. Huh, funny how he remembered *those* details. Still, the truck sure was a beauty. And *way* out of his league. When he inherited the ranch he had promised himself that one day, when the business started making a healthy profit, he would get the biggest, baddest truck there was, and that F-350 was it. Whoever owned that beast was a lucky SOB.

"That's a nice-looking truck," Trey murmured, struggling to keep the envy out of his voice.

Greta bit her lip, fighting back a grin. "I know. That's what you said when you brought it home. And after every time you wash it, and wax it, and pull it out of the driveway."

"That's mine?" No way. He jumped out of the SUV to get a better look.

When his dad had run the ranch, they'd had enough money for the essentials but not enough to splurge on massive vehicles. Damn, he must be doing pretty well.

Or else he was horrible when it came to finances and they were deep in the hole. Please let him be a ranching genius.

He couldn't resist walking up to the silver monster and brushing some of the dust off of the emblem with his shirttail.

"That man and his truck." Greta laughed.

Mark chuckled with her. "Hey, I'm going to make a call into the hands. Do you need anything?"

Trey might have been enthralled with his truck, but he caught the meaningful look Mark leveled at Greta.

"No. I think we're okay. You will be by for dinner, right?" There was a quiver in her voice.

"Sure, sure. I'll be by in a few." He held his hand out to Trey. After they shook, Mark pulled him in for a two-slap pat on his uninjured shoulder. "Good to have you back, Hoss."

"Good to be back."

The statement was true. It was good. He was back on his land with his best friend and a beautiful woman by his side. What more did he need?

Oh right, his memory.

"Ready to go inside, or should I give you two some time to get reacquainted?" She looked from him to the truck with a questioning quirk of her brow.

He liked her sense of humor. "I think she'll survive without me for a little bit."

Trey followed Greta through the garage and into the cool interior of the house. The ground floor was laid out to flow in a circular pattern. He knew that if he turned to his right, the hallway led to the living room. A left in there led down the hall past his office, then onto the dining room, the kitchen, and finally back to the garage. All right. One more memory down. He was on a roll.

"Feel familiar?" Greta asked when they reached the foyer.

"Yeah, it does." And again, it didn't.

The white walls and dark wood trim were the same from his childhood, but the furniture was much more modern with leather couches and a flat screen TV. While the room was beautiful, it felt more like a showroom. Cold, informal, and quiet. Museum quiet.

"I don't see how we manage to keep the living room looking so nice when it must get destroyed when the hands come over for *Monday Night Football*."

"Ah, yeah. Well, they haven't done that in a long while. Come on, I'll show you what we've done upstairs since we've been married."

What? No *Monday Night Football*? When he was a kid, Monday had been his favorite night of the week, sitting by his dad's chair, brushing potato chips out of his hair and screaming at the television when those SOB Broncos stopped the Hawks. It had been on a Super Bowl Sunday that he and Mark had their first beer. Boy had his mom been pissed when she found out his dad had been the one to give the eighteen year-olds a bottle to share.

He frowned at Greta's back as he followed her up the stairs. Maybe she wasn't a sports fan and the weekly revelry had moved to one of the bunkhouses. That was the only logical explanation.

"This is where I work," Greta said as she ushered him into one of the bedrooms.

Two long tables with racks of small trays underneath met in the far corner. Beads in various colors and sizes lay scattered across the surface besides pliers and spools of fine wire. Along the opposite wall was a day bed heaped with pillows.

"I make jewelry." She gestured with quiet pride to a necklace sitting on display that appeared to be in mid-production. The blue and silver beads sparkled in the sunlight spilling in through the window.

"That's beautiful," he marveled. "Where did you get all of the beads?" He picked up an earring made with blood red teardrops. He imagined Greta wearing the jewelry and nothing else. The image of the bright color lying against her delicate neck made him clear his throat.

"I make them." She stood near the door with her hands tucked into her back pockets. She shifted from one foot to the other.

"Really? Wow. That's amazing." The intricate knot work in the wire and the shapes of the pieces of glass showed off her talent. "I've never met anyone who's artistic before. Well, except you, of course."

"I know." Her chuckle seemed to suggest she was laughing

at a private joke. "Come on." She jerked her head toward the door. She led him to the room at the end of the hall. "And here is the bedroom."

He noticed that she hadn't said "our room," but he kept his mouth shut.

A big bed took up the middle of the white-walled room. The worn quilt and the fluffy pillows looked inviting. He was half tempted to ask Greta to take a nap with him, but took another glance around.

Strong lines, tidy, nothing fancy. The room even smelled familiar. Musky with a hint of the spicy aftershave he'd been wearing since he was in high school.

In the walk-in closet, his work shirts hung alongside Greta's sundresses. He liked seeing their clothes together. It made their connection more real.

Greta gestured to her right. "The bathroom is through there." She took a position near the door and didn't seem inclined to venture far from the spot.

He walked in only to draw up short. "Now this is different."

The cream tiled floor and Jacuzzi tub had definitely not been there when this had been his parents' space. Visions of him and Greta relaxing under the jetted sprays after a long day's work filled his mind. Trey blinked rapidly to clear his head. *Focus, concentrate on the here and now*, he reminded his body. They'd make it there eventually.

As he turned back to the bedroom, something struck him as being all wrong. The manly room was just that. Manly. Where was the jewelry spread across the dresser? Why weren't there picture frames set out, or makeup littering the bathroom counter? Except for the clothes in the closet, nothing indicated that Greta lived there too.

He eyed her protective stance near the door and tamped

down his frustration. Her eyes darted everywhere as her weight shifted from one hip to the other. Hesitancy he could understand, but she was acting downright fearful. Down the back of his neck his skin tingled with warning, much like the way a horse tensed when sensing a predator approach. The world was not as it should be.

Well, if he was going to get his memory of her back, now seemed like a good time to start asking questions. "So. This is our room?"

Her brow crinkled with confusion and she tilted her head. "Yep." One foot was pointed toward the door as if ready to bolt.

He nodded and relaxed his stance, measuring his breath in and out, deep and even. He hooked his thumb into his belt loops and lowered his shoulders as if nothing was amiss. She was just like a wild animal and he didn't want to startle her with any sudden movement. "You're either very tidy, or you don't spend a whole lot of time in here."

Her breath lodged in her throat and made a small strangling sound. "What does that mean?"

"It means that for a woman as creative as you, I would think there'd be a more feminine touch in here."

She snorted and planted her hands on her hips. "You know how busy it gets around here. Like I have time to decorate."

"Your workroom has your personality all over it. That looks like a place you'd spend all of your time in."

Her eyes widened before she shut down all expression, but he saw the flinch nonetheless. His oh-shit meter began to climb. "Is that what you do? Spend all day in there? Do you—do you sleep in that tiny bed?"

"Sometimes." She shrugged casually, but the way she suddenly found the carpet interesting suggested that it was more often than sometimes.

"That's just ridiculous." And entirely unbelievable.

There was no way in hell he'd allow his woman to sleep in a dinky little bed. Even if she had fallen asleep in her workroom, he would have scooped her up to cuddle with through the night. What did that say about him as a husband to leave her cramped and alone while he slept in a king-sized bed large enough for a lot of lovin'?

"Trey, it's no big deal." She forced a laugh and edged closer to the door. "You know how it is on the ranch. Things happen at all hours of the night. You're not always home either."

Why the hell not? His dad made it home every night, because family was just as important as the land. What kind of a husband *was* he?

"Well, that's changing. This is our home and our bed, and we are going to sleep in it like a normal married couple."

"Trey, it's not important."

"It is to me. It's my job to provide for you, and that means giving you a comfortable bed to rest in."

"Trey, really—"

"No! Damn it, Greta." He took a step toward her.

She backed up so fast she bounced against the wall. Her body trembled, her eyes widened with fear, yet she was braced for violence that she seemed to expect.

Trey stopped short as an icy wave washed over him. *Good God.*

No. No. It wasn't possible. His throat seized but he forced out the words. "Jesus, Greta. Have I hurt you?"

Greta's jaw dropped. "What? No." She shook her head. "No. You've never hit me."

You've never hit me. But he had hurt her. The shaking, the protective stance, the rapid breathing, all screamed it. The knowledge that he had caused this woman harm twisted in his chest like a hot branding iron.

"I'm sorry, Greta. I didn't mean to come at you. I'm not

going to hurt you." Hurting a woman, any woman, went against everything he had ever been taught to believe about what it meant to be a man.

"It's not that, Trey–" She stopped and pressed her face into her hands. He gave her all the time she needed to pull her thoughts together. She kept her hands folded in front of her mouth as she looked up at him with those big brown eyes filled with regret, sympathy, and a whole lot of confusion. "I don't know. I just don't know." With agitated hands she brushed the loose tendrils of hair off her face. "I don't know how I'm supposed to act or what to expect of you. I didn't mean to make you feel bad about the bed. I just, I just don't know what to do."

She looked as helpless as he felt. How do you pick up a life you knew nothing about? "Don't be afraid of me. Please, just don't be afraid." The plea came out low and rough.

The tension seeped from her shoulders as she took a deep breath. "I'm not afraid of you."

"I sincerely hope not, Greta." He spread out his arms to encompass the room. "This just all feels strange to me, and I know you're just as lost too. What am I missing? What's the biggest thing I'm forgetting that I need to know now? I can't stumble around blind like this. I don't want to hurt you by saying something insensitive on accident. Please, help me out."

Greta sucked in a breath as if he'd punched her in the stomach. Her eyes clouded with grief as she blinked back tears.

"Um." She swallowed twice and looked everywhere but at him.

Trey felt his breathing escalate along with hers as she struggled against an imaginary panic and his oh-shit meter rang again.

She had to clear her throat before she found the voice to answer, and even then the sound was rough. "We had a son. His name was Luke. He passed away over a year ago. He was two."

Chapter 4

"*F*UCK,"EXPLODED FROM Trey's lips. He swayed on his feet and braced a hand on the nearby dresser at the news that rocked him to the core.

Just brand the word *Asshole* across his forehead right now. First, he couldn't remember his wife, then his own child? A child who had passed away?

And Greta. Poor Greta had to live the loss all over again in order to remind him.

"Jesus, Greta. I'm sorry. I didn't—ah, fuck." He clenched and unclenched his fists then clutched at his shirt as if he could physically keep his racing heart from leaping out of his chest.

"No, Trey, no." She placed a soothing hand on his bicep. "I figured you might not..." She swallowed again. "I probably should have told you sooner, but I couldn't. I just couldn't. Please. I understand. It's—it's uh"—another swallow—"you've had a lot to deal with lately."

Her sympathy was appreciated, but it didn't stop him from feeling like the shittiest man on the planet. Forgetting your own child was unforgivable. Absolutely no excuse.

Now the root of Greta's anxiety was clear. Any minute, she must have expected him to remember Luke or be faced with the moment when she'd have to remind him. No wonder she'd been so damn cagey.

A million questions flooded his mind. How did their son die? Oh God, did he play a part?

Did he want to know the answers?

The sorrow on her face ate at his gut. She lived with the pain of losing a child every day. He'd only had four minutes. Was he ready to rip open a wound he hadn't known existed until that moment? Did he want to force Greta to tell the tale when they were still on shaky ground?

To drop the subject might be a cowardly move, but he wasn't ready to listen, and it appeared as if she wasn't ready to talk. Later. Later he'd ask. But his wife needed him now.

"I'm so sorry, Greta." This time he didn't hesitate to take her hand. "I'm going to remember. You and Luke." Luke. He liked that name. "I will remember," he vowed. "Look, I don't want to hurt you anymore. I can stay somewhere else. Maybe in one of the bunkhouses."

"Trey. Stop it." The strength in her voice shocked him. "This is your home. You've been hurt and need to heal. This is where you belong. Let's not worry about the past. Concentrate on now."

One step, then another brought her flush against him. She was so soft, so lush. He could hold her all day. Trey held every muscle still, waiting to see what she'd do next.

Her arms came up slowly to encircle his neck. As her head rested against his chest, the breath he held came out in a rush, ruffling her hair.

Trey wrapped his arms around her waist and hugged her tight. Probably tighter than he should, but she felt so good in his embrace. Soft, woman, home. She was his only real link to his past. His anchor. They were connected, bonded. He knew it, he felt it. Like the warm solid beat in his chest, he knew in his heart that she belonged to him.

Her fingers threaded through his hair. He knew the gesture was meant to comfort, but it had his nerves vibrating on so many different levels it made him shake. Her breath hitched when she felt the row of stitches that ran down the back of his scalp. "I'm sorry you got hurt." The softly spoken words wobbled. "I never wanted—I—" she broke off and pressed closer, burying her face into his shirt.

"Hey, hey," he soothed. "I'm okay. Nothing that time won't fix." Moisture pooled in his own eyes, and he blinked it away.

This overwhelming uncertainty was so fucking frustrating. He was a bubbling volcano of want. He wanted to take the solace she offered, wanted to kiss those lips until they turned dark pink with desire, wanted to stay just like they were until their legs gave out and they fell to the floor. Want, want, want. Take, take, take.

He might be her husband, but it didn't sit right with him to take such liberties. No matter how fierce the need was to remember their past and pick up where they might have left off, he'd just have to reconcile himself to the fact that his brain would not be rushed. Until that time came, he would have to do his best to do right by Greta.

"I'm sorry I got angry about the bed," he murmured into her neck. "I don't like the thought that you ever felt like you couldn't sleep in your own bed. My wife should be happy."

"I understand." Her sigh carried the weight of the world. Some of the rigidity returned to her spine as she visibly braced herself and said, "Sometimes we don't always see eye to eye. We may fight big, but we love big too. We're not the most perfect couple," she admitted with a tiny chuckle. "I know you have so much on your mind, Trey. Please, don't force it. We just need to adjust. Remember, one day at a time. We've been through worse."

Like the death of their son. Trey didn't think that anything would ever make up for him not being able to remember his child.

When her body shifted to step back, he tightened his hold. He felt her cheek bunch against his chest as she smiled in response.

"I'm going to let you have some privacy. I need to check on dinner, too."

Trey didn't want to let her go, but he knew she was right. They both probably needed a moment alone. She gave him a tremulous smile and brushed her thumb over his cheek before she left him on his own with one of her signature shy smiles. The sensation of her touch lingered long after she'd gone.

In the wake of her absence, a deafening silence rolled into the empty room. A terrible, thrown-into-a raging-river sensation of helplessness swamped over him like a tidal wave.

"Damn it," he muttered as he ran his hands through his hair.

He had to fix this. Somehow, he was going to have to try to make up for the last few days and chase the cloud of pain from Greta's eyes. Try to be her husband.

No.

Determination straightened his spine. He *was* her husband. There would be no trying about it. All he had to do was suck it up and be the husband he knew he could be.

She said they weren't the perfect couple. Well, who was? He had to stop worrying about the past. Focus on the present and everything would fall into place.

"Right." He pulled on his cuffs and stood taller. "You can do this."

The air conditioner kicked on, blasting out a cold stream of air that reminded him a bit too much of his time in the hospital. Fresh air and hard-packed earth under his boots was just what he needed to get his bearings.

As he headed toward the stairs, he passed the door of what he knew had been his room as a child. Greta hadn't shown him inside, and he wondered if it was decorated with the same blue and tan gingham of his youth or if it had been converted into a guest room.

He reached for the doorknob and his hand froze millimeters from the gold-plated knob. A thousand alarms screamed in his head at him to not open the door as a sense of dread crawled up his chest and tightened his throat. The soles of his boots shuffled across the carpet as he stumbled a step back and looked at the door in confusion.

Maybe he needed the fresh air more than he thought.

Shaking off the disturbing reaction, he ran down the stairs and out the front door into the dry climate. He could have gone out the back, through the mudroom near the kitchen, but he wanted to give Greta some space.

The hot summer air slapped him in the face as he stepped outside and made the walk around the house toward the barns. Glittering like a gemstone in the late afternoon sun, his silver truck came into view and he stopped to admire the clean lines and sheer size of the monster. Boy, was she pretty. Did he and Greta ever take drives out into the hills with a cooler of beers and an air mattress in the flat bed?

The image of Greta, naked and straddling his waist with the stars dancing above them, made his cock swell and his temperature jump. Man, he really needed to focus on not getting aroused every time he thought about her. If he wasn't careful, he was going to embarrass himself more than he already had.

He turned from the truck to head toward the barn and

hoped the earthy scent of the stalls would help relieve the intense swelling that caused him to walk funny.

Behind the hills, the sun was setting in a brilliant ball of orange and pink. Entranced by the swirl of color, Trey stepped up to the corral and rested his foot on the bottom rail of the fence to admire its beauty. During this time of the year almost the entire herd was deep in the hills, feeding for the summer, which left the paddock before him empty save for the few heifers that were too ill or too weak to make the journey. Their tails flicked in short snaps as they ignored his presence.

Now this—*this* he remembered. A summer sunset dusting the rocky hillsides with a rosy blush meant the end of a day of hard labor and the promise of supper time and talks around the fire pit, or maybe a game of catch in the driveway with some of the hands. This was home.

Nearby a door slammed shut and Mark walked out of the open side of the horse barn.

"Hey," Trey greeted.

Mark nodded. "Hey." He adjusted the tilt of his black cowboy hat. The color matched his closely cropped hair.

"Everything check out all right?" Trey asked.

His friend's lips twitched. "They're cows and they're eating. Not much more exciting than that." He ambled over and copied Trey's stance. "I have the boys working on mending the fence lines. The last of the alfalfa's been harvested. It's been pretty quiet."

As Mark filled him in on the status and particulars of the rest of the ranch, Trey felt his eyes widened and gave a low whistle. "I'm doing pretty well."

"You sure are, Hoss."

"I have a feeling that you've had a big hand in that."

Mark smiled. "You'd be correct."

"By the way, you're Hoss. I'm Little Joe, remember?"

"Whatever you say, Hoss." Mark winked, continuing the battle that had raged between them since they were twelve and spent their weekends in a little shed his father had turned into a clubhouse for them. They had a little black and white television with rabbit ear antennae that picked up one channel that ran all day marathons of *Bonanza* and *Wagon Train*. It wasn't much, but they it was all their own.

Trey laughed and turned back to the sunset. He licked his lips and drew a deep breath. Pause, pause, pause. "Greta…Greta seems pretty great." Was that a subtle-enough transition?

Mark shot him a sideways glance. "Greta *is* great. You lucked out when you married her." He reached into his pocket and pulled out a pack of cigarettes.

Trey frowned. "Since when do you smoke?"

Mark looked at him in surprise as he lit up. "Since when did you stop?"

His eyebrows shot up. "I smoke?"

"Naw." Mark chuckled and exhaled a long stream of smoke. "I thought if I said you did, you might join me."

"No way, Hoss. Hey, blow it that way, man." He shook his head then looked out into the distance.

Both men went quiet as they watched the landscape turn soft purple in the waning light. In the barn, the wood slats of the stall creaked as a horse leaned its heavy weight against the wall. A fly brushed past Trey's ear, the buzz sending a tiny shiver down his back. Mark stubbed the end of his cigarette into the fence and placed the butt into his front pocket. Trey looked back at the house, then out toward the horizon again.

"Are Greta and I good?" He finally gave voice to the question that had been burning a hole in his gut.

Mark tensed. His oldest friend threw him that wary sideways

glance of his. "What do you mean?"

"I mean, do we get along and do we, you know," he jerked his head left and right, "get along?"

Mark let out a long breath and tilted his hat lower over his eyes. "I try to make it a point not to meddle in other people's lives. Especially relationships. Why don't you ask your wife?"

Trey scowled. "I don't want her even more frightened of me."

Mark's gaze narrowed. "Why is she frightened?"

"She's not frightened–frightened." Damn, he was fucking this up. "She's just uncertain about me. You know, about where my head is at, or not at. I don't want her to feel like she needs to tell me what she thinks I want to hear. You'll give it to me true. Right?"

With his long fingers he withdrew another cigarette and lit it with a deft flick of the wrist. All the while, that steady black gaze never wavered. "Greta is the best thing that ever happened to you. You struck gold with that one."

Okay, so Greta was a treasure, but nothing about how Trey treated her or how they were as a couple.

"She's been great, considering. Her jewelry is amazing. Never thought I'd marry an artsy type."

Mark let go with a snort of laughter.

"She's…she's, uh, really pretty." The only response to that was a raised eyebrow. "She's hot, man," he admitted, digging the toe of his boot into the dirt and feeling like a dirty horn dog.

"Trey, are you wondering if it's okay to have the hots for your wife?"

He grimaced. "For all intents and purposes, I just met her. I shouldn't have such husbandly feelings yet."

"Hoss, I cannot talk to you about this." Mark shook his head. "Just take it easy there."

"I'm trying."

A harsh clanging sound echoed across the field.

"Boys!" Greta called from the back porch. "Dinner's ready."

"Be right in." Mark stubbed out his cigarette. "Look, I'm not faulting you one bit, but Greta's been through a lot too, you know. Just take it slow."

Trey wholeheartedly agreed. She lost her son and in a way, her husband. She definitely didn't need to add his hormones to the mix.

Both men stopped in the mudroom to wash up on their way to the dining room. A cloud of rosemary, garlic, and roasting beef wafted in from the kitchen and set their stomachs to rumble.

"God." Trey inhaled deep and closed his eyes in bliss. "Whatever that is smells so good."

"That's why she's the cook." Mark smiled. "I think you proposed to her the first time she made you breakfast." He rolled his sleeves over his elbows and started soaping up his arms.

"You getting ready to perform surgery there, Hoss?" Trey commented while watching the scrub down.

He shrugged. "Greta doesn't like it when I come in smelling of smoke."

Weird how he didn't remember Mark ever smoking and wondered what led him to start the habit. When they were younger, Mark was the voice of reason. Oh, they did their share of stupid shit, but Mark was the one to point out the less dangerous, or illegal, way to raise hell. They both loved their mothers too much to make them cry. Now seeing his friend with a vice disturbed him. Just what else had he forgotten?

From what Trey had been told earlier, the rest of the ranch hands had made other dining arrangements, so it was only the three of them for the evening meal. Trey took his place at the head of the table and his mouth watered as he eyed the feast of pot roast, mashed potatoes, and roasted carrots Greta prepared for his homecoming. After days of IV drips and hospital food, he was ready to tear into a hunk of meat as if he were a crazed animal.

The first tender bite of roast melted on his tongue, and he could believe Mark's comment that he proposed to Greta the first time he had tasted her cooking. For several long minutes, the only sounds in the room were of utensils scraping against the china and appreciative murmurs.

After the edge of his hunger wore down, Trey finally took the bull by the horns and started a conversation no one seemed eager to begin. "Do you have family around here, Greta?"

"No, not anymore. I grew up near Seattle, and my parents are still out there. I had a cousin who was going to school near here. She was the reason I came to Mission in the first place. She recently moved to the Tri-Cities area."

"So, it's just you, me, and all of the hands? Any girlfriends you hang out with?"

"I have a few. I'm pretty busy."

He paused to take a drink. "How are your folks, Mark?" Mark's parents owned the feed store in Mission, the closest town to the ranch.

"Mom's good. She likes living out in Tacoma."

"When did she move out there?"

"After my dad died."

"What?" His dad died? "When? How?"

"About four years ago. Sorry. I didn't know if you remembered that or not." The corner of his mouth kicked up. "Don't look so surprised. The man smoked two packs a day and ate nothing but steak for breakfast, lunch, and dinner. It wasn't too much of a shock when his heart gave out."

"I'm sorry. I didn't mean to bring up sad memories. I seem to be doing that a lot today."

Mark looked over at Great who gave an almost imperceptible shake of her head before glancing at her plate. Mark's mouth tightened as he too lowered his head.

A forkful of creamy mashed potatoes turned into a lump of flavorless nothing in his mouth as Trey understood what they hadn't said. He didn't remember Luke.

Although he had no control over his memories, the shame over not remembering his own flesh and blood left him numb.

"Greta, that was great." Mark rubbed his stomach in appreciation and pushed away from the table. "We'll clean-up for you."

"You don't have to do that." She reached for the heavy platter of roast beef.

Trey jumped to his feet and snatched the platter away. "No trouble, magpie, we can handle it."

Greta and Mark froze. Ever so slowly she raised her shocked gaze to his. The sudden stillness in the room kick started his heart and made his blood pump loudly in his ears. "What is it?"

"You called me magpie. Why?"

"I don't know. Was that wrong?"

"No." She swallowed hard. "You just haven't called me that in a long while." She looked at him with that wary tilt of her head. "Are you remembering anything else?"

He had no idea why he called her that. The nickname just slipped out. He tried to force his brain to remember more, but all that did was give him a headache.

"I've got nothing."

Greta released a slow breath, her posture deflating. In fact, the whole room felt like a balloon that had all of the air let out.

"It's all right. One day at a time, right?"

"Yeah." He didn't sound so sure.

Mark pushed her toward the door. "Go on and relax. Your kitchen is in good hands."

She passed a small smile to Trey before leveling a fierce glare at the much taller man. "It better be, or no waffles in the morning."

Mark's dark eyes lit up. "With berries?"

She drew back, affronted. "Of course."

Mark let go with a low whistle before he turned to Trey. "Well, come on, Hoss. Let's not waste time."

Trey helped stack dishes in the sink as Mark started washing. Years of growing up at their mamas' side in the kitchen had honed their cleaning skills. They worked silently, Mark not being much of a talker, and Trey afraid of opening his mouth. It seemed like every time he did, he reopened some horrible wound.

As he worked, he kept his ears open, listening for any sound of movement in the house.

Mark chuckled and threw a dishtowel at his head. "She's out on the swing."

Trey grimaced at his transparency. "How do you know?"

"Because she likes to sit on the swing. Go on out there. I can finish the last of this."

"Are you sure?" He was willing to pull his weight, but he *really* wanted to spend more time with Greta.

"Please, get outta here. Oh, wait." He reached for an open bottle of wine on the counter and poured a measure into a goblet. "Take a glass of this." He handed it to him with a wink. "She likes to have one after dinner. Antioxidants, she claims."

"Thanks, Hoss."

With the offering cradled in his palm, he set out to find

Greta. The swing on the wide wraparound porch was his mom's favorite spot on the ranch. It was fitting that it was also his wife's.

He approached her on quiet feet, entranced again by her beauty and the calm serenity that wrapped around her as she gazed out into the inky darkness. "Would you like some company?"

The soft illumination coming from the porch light cast part of her face in shadow. What he could see of her smiled at him in welcome. "Sure."

"Here, this is for you."

She looked from him to the glass in surprise. "How did—"

"Mark told me," he confessed with a sheepish grin. "Said something about the oxygen."

She laughed. "Thank you." She took the glass and scooted over. "Have a seat."

The swing creaked and jostled with his added weight, then quickly fell into a smooth rhythm. Long minutes passed while they sat in companionable silence. The tranquility should have lulled him into a drowsy slumber, but the butterflies in his stomach turned into stampeding bulls and settled in his chest at the thought of what he was about to do. There was never going to be a right time, so now was just as good as any.

He wet his lips and released a breath. "Greta. Can you tell me about Luke?"

Chapter 5

GRETA TOOK A long sip of wine, and Trey's blood pressure rose as he watched the flex of her elegant throat. The tip of her tongue swept a stray drop off her lip, almost—almost—distracting him from his line of questioning before she set the glass down by her feet. She turned her whole body toward him, presenting herself like an open book. "What do you want to know?"

The breath he held whooshed out. "Everything. I feel horrible that I don't even remember my own son."

She placed her hand over his and squeezed, her smile quivering around the edges. "He was a hell-raiser in training, just like his daddy. When he was born, he didn't cry after that first breath of air. He just blinked those big baby blues of his at us then fell right to sleep. We were convinced he was going to be the most agreeable baby." She laughed. "We were so wrong. Luke cried whenever we weren't with him. It got so bad we took turns sleeping upright with him in our arms. The moment he learned how to stand, he'd crawl out of his crib. You started calling him 'Ninja Luke' after he woke you up one morning by hitting you in the face with a sippy cup. He gave the biggest hugs and the sloppiest kisses and drove us insane."

Greta's smile faded as she turned to look out into the night. "One day I put him down for a nap. He didn't wake up. The doctor said he had an aneurysm in his brain. It was nothing we would have seen or done something to prevent. Supposedly it was quick and he didn't feel any pain, or so they said. He came into this world quietly, and he left the same way."

Trey didn't know if it was a blessing or a curse to not remember Luke as she did. The terror they must have faced while watching an innocent soul pass on for no reason. The pain had to be unimaginable and he was sorry that Greta had to relive the grief to tell him.

Her image swam in his vision and a boulder-sized ball of hurt settled on his chest. He had to do something to ease the sorrow etched in the tight line of her lips. "Can I hold you?"

She nodded and scooted closer. Her breathing was deep and even as she tried to hold herself together. He saw the glisten of a tear as it traced a shimmering path down her cheek.

Just as she was about to rest her head against his chest, she pulled back. "Your shoulder."

"It's fine." His palm slid around her nape to guide her back down. "I'm sore, but fine. Just come here." With his good arm he reached under her knees and pulled her legs around so that they rested across his lap. When her arms hugged him around his middle, he took it as an invitation to gather her closer and stroke his hands in a soothing swirl over her back. "Tell me your happiest memory of Luke."

"Oh." She breathed out in a long sigh. "He so loved you." There was awe and wonder in her tone. "He could tell your footsteps from everyone else's. I'd hear a set of boots on the porch. 'Is that Daddy?' I'd ask. 'No.' He'd shake his head. Then another set would come along. 'That's Daddy.' He was right every time."

"It sounds like he was pretty smart. But he'd have to be if he came from you and me."

Greta looked up at him with a startled smile, as if she were astounded he would find enjoyment in her memories.

"I hate making you sad, Greta. You don't have to talk about Luke anymore."

"I want to. I want to talk about him with you. It was horrible, and I wouldn't wish that on anybody. Even though he was only with us for a short time, he was ours, and we loved him. I wouldn't give that up for anything."

He ran his hand down the length of her hair. Her compassion and strength amazed him. "That's the important thing."

Greta's eyes narrowed. "Yes. Yes, it is." The seriousness in her tone gave him pause.

Family had always meant the world to him. Whether it was the one he had grown up in, or the one born of friendship. He'd do anything to protect what was his, or so he'd believed in his youth. By her response, he had to wonder if he still held onto that belief.

Unable to stop himself, he touched her hair again. The silken weight of it grounded him in the here and now. He became very aware that he sat in the near dark with a beautiful woman in his arms, sharing a very intimate moment. His body hardened and softened at the same time, and he pulled her a fraction of an inch closer. They were connected by a memory of sorrow, and Trey wanted a link of something good.

"Tell me about our first kiss."

"Wow." Her brows rose. "You change gears quickly." Her soft chuckle made his breath hitch and his fingers tightened where they had landed on her hip. He was pleased when he felt an answering shudder race through her.

He shrugged. "I'm curious about you. About us. I want to

hear about something happy."

"You think our first kiss was a happy memory?"

"It wasn't?" How could it not have been?

Greta threw her head back and laughed long and hard. Her hair rippled down her back and her shoulders shook as he stared at her with both confusion and amusement. It was the first time he had earned a genuine smile from her and he wanted to do it again.

"Our first kiss." She sobered and bit her lip as her gaze focused inward. This time when she laughed it was with a low and husky purr. It poured over him like syrup and pooled in his groin. "We'd been dancing, and you were trying to convince me that I was your girl. You pulled a macho move and planted one on me as I was trying to walk away. It was the funniest thing ever."

"Why was it funny?"

"Because it was all soft and lippy and really wet. I was surprised that the great love-'em-and-leave-'em Trey Armstrong was a piss-poor kisser." She giggled.

"That can't be right." He looked away in disbelief and shifted in his seat. "You must be remembering it wrong."

"*You're* questioning *my* memory?"

"Well, yeah." He didn't recall having any troubles where the ladies were concerned. She must be playing with him. "I couldn't have been that bad. You obviously stuck with me."

"I had to retrain you."

Retrain him, huh? "Was I a quick study?" he smirked.

Her expression took on a dreamy quality that had him thinking of hot summer nights tangled in crisp cool sheets. "Yeah, you were."

He leaned in close, close enough to smell the wine on her breath. It was impossible to take his eyes off her succulent lips.

"Do you think I still remember how?"

Greta's eyes widened at the unspoken request in his query. "You'd have to tell me," she whispered.

He dipped his head ever so slowly. Watching, waiting to see if she'd pull away. Her gaze fell to his lips, making them tingle in anticipation until he pressed his mouth to hers. Remembering her "soft lips" comment, he kept his touch firm. When he felt her smile in response, he slanted his mouth over hers and coaxed her to open for him.

She gasped and melted in his embrace, her arms slipping around his neck to hold on tight. She tasted of wine and spice, and he wanted more. Her little whimpers pushed the need to claim her to the breaking point, twisting and twisting until he thought he would snap.

Hot damn. Her kiss burned him to the core. If he could, he'd crawl inside her and not leave for days. His shaft throbbed and reminded him that it had been awhile since he had engaged in any vigorous activity. Since he couldn't remember the last time he had had a taste of her body, it felt how like he suspected he had the first time with her, hot desperate and completely out of control. Which was why he needed to stop. Now.

The need to take her slow, then fast, then slow again was strong. But the need to have her trust was greater. She was holding back. He felt it. Any information about their relationship he'd had to coax from her like getting a newborn calf to accept a new mama. She hadn't refused to answer his questions, but she hadn't elaborated, either. For some reason she was hiding something, and that bothered him.

With a strength he didn't know he possessed, he tore away, leaving them both struggling for breath.

Her lips were swollen and wet, her eyes dazed as she blinked up at him. "Yeah, you remembered," she said as she exhaled.

"I'm not gonna lie to you, Greta." His throat was so raw it hurt. "I want you. Want you something fierce. From the moment I first saw you, you called to me. My head might not remember you, but my body sure does."

His fingertips traced a path down her cheek to settle around her throat. Her skin felt like silk against his callused palm, and her pulse beat in a frantic rhythm. Her lips parted with a startled gasp at his possessive touch, and her breasts pressed deeper into his chest.

"As much as I'd love to set you up on that railing there and fly us both to the moon, I'm gonna do my damnedest to restrain myself. I have the feeling the man I am today isn't the same man I remember being. I think we both need a little time to adjust."

Her sharp intake of breath and sudden stillness confirmed his suspicions. He hated the possibility that he had hurt his woman. Somehow he was going to make it up to her. "Now tomorrow, I'm not making any promises about tomorrow. Why don't you go on and get ready for bed. I'll be up in a bit."

Seconds passed while she gazed into his eyes. He stared back, his thumb stroking over her collarbone. He wished he knew what she was looking for and wished even more that she'd find it.

"Okay," she said. The muscles in her thighs flexed as she prepared to stand, but she shifted and hugged him tight. "I'm glad you're back," she whispered in his ear.

Trey hid his smile while he watched her walk away on shaky legs. As soon as the door closed behind her, he doubled over and pressed his hand against his throbbing erection.

"Geez-us," he groaned. No wonder why he had married her. A woman who could cook like an angel and kiss like a demon should not be left unclaimed.

One kiss, one scorching kiss, and he was ready to come long

and hard. How would it be when he finally had her naked and underneath him? "I'm in deep shit," he muttered.

For half a second he considered rubbing out a quick one, but only for half a second. With his luck, he'd get caught by one of the hands, or worse, Greta, and that would be sad.

He stood on his own wobbly legs and took a slow walk around the house, twice, before he ventured back inside.

Greta was exiting the bathroom just as he entered the bedroom. She wore a satin tank top and matching shorts in bubble gum pink. The material cupped and hugged her curves in all the places his hands itched to cover. She looked fresh, tousled, and sexy as hell.

"Enjoy your walk?" Amusement flirted around her lips.

"Get under the covers before I break my promise," he warned. He liked this sassy side of her, maybe a little too much. Her smart mouth had the blood rushing back to his groin. With her hips rolling in a seductive sway as she walked to the bed, *their* bed, he was never more tempted to break a promise than he was right then.

He couldn't watch as she crawled onto the mattress. If he saw her bent over with her satin-covered ass in the air, he would be on her in a heartbeat.

Trey snatched up a pair of shorts and escaped into the bathroom. Safely away from temptation, he tried to cool his blood by splashing cold water on his face.

He turned the water off with a rough twist of his wrist. "Ah, fuck it."

In seconds, he was stripped and in the shower.

Trey swore he heard her laughter coming from the other room as the stinging-cold needles of water sluiced over him. When he was numb from the neck down, he got out and briskly dried off. He had to bite his lip to keep from groaning at the feel of the cotton against his over-sensitized skin.

In the bedroom, Greta left one light on in welcome. She had followed his directions and was already in bed. Her dark hair spilled over the pillow like molasses. The thought of it covering his chest the same way had him shaking his head to clear the desire away.

He turned the light off and dove under the covers to spoon behind her. He said he wasn't going to have sex with her, but that didn't mean he would miss the opportunity to hold her all night long.

Trey slid one arm under her head and the other around her waist. His broad palm rested along her belly, warming the fabric of her top with his heat. The effects of the cold shower vanished at her nearness. He didn't bother trying to fight it anymore. It was too exhausting. Instead, he pulled her closer and let her feel his hard length against her back. Greta tensed as if waiting for him to cop a feel. He was her husband. He had every right to at least try to make a move, but he'd made a promise. It was a stupid promise, but it was still a promise. He needed her trust, and he needed her to share. She probably knew him better than anyone, and that connection would help him find his way back from the void.

Little by little, he felt her muscles ease until she fell asleep in his arms. Only then did he relax and sink deeper into the pillows. He stuck his nose in her hair and inhaled. Jasmine and vanilla. This was what he wanted his bed to smell like every night.

Unable to resist, he lifted her hand and stared at the ring on her third finger. A tiny diamond winked at him in the moonlight streaming in from the window, a good indication of his financial status at the time of his proposal. The braided gold band was a delicate counterpart to the masculine version of his ring. A matched set.

"What's this?" he mumbled and leaned forward for a better look.

While he had been admiring their rings, Greta's was a little loose and had slipped up her finger, exposing an area of skin that was the same peachy color as the rest of her hand. He wiggled his own ring and the pale area of flesh beneath the metal practically glowed white in the dim light. The lack of a tan line on Greta's finger wasn't necessarily a portent of bad news, but he couldn't scratch the itch there was a deeper meaning hidden there.

Did he want to know what it was?

Chapter 6

TREY WOKE UP the next morning hungry, horny, and alone. The hunger and horniness he expected, but he was saddened by the alone part. Greta's side of the bed was stone cold, suggesting that she'd been gone for a while. What time was it? The bedside clock flashed eight o'clock. Mid-morning by ranching standards, but not slacker late.

He stretched out his limbs as far as he could reach. His toes and fingertips touched all four corners of the king-sized bed. The muscles around his shoulder protested the movement, making him grimace. He was sore and achy, but felt fully confident he could accomplish any task he needed to, however, he'd take it easy, just like he promised. The hospital had given him the creeps, and he didn't want to risk going back because he felt he had something to prove.

Rolling over, he buried his face deep in her pillow. Greta's scent lingered, sending the blood rushing through his body. It was even better than the smell of cows.

Greta and...bacon?

"Oh God, she's cooking," he groaned. His mouth watered with anticipation.

In a flash, he was up and out of bed. He dressed and ran out of the room so fast he was still tucking his blue work shirt into his jeans when he reached the bottom of the stairs.

The deep rumble of voices drifted down the hall. Judging by the sound of laughter, it appeared his men were happy and in high spirits.

As he approached the kitchen, a feminine voice chimed in and hardy male laughter responded. He stopped in the doorway to observe the scene before him.

When this was his mother's kitchen, she had had two shabby refrigerators and worked her tail off to feed eight hungry men. Since then, the equipment had been upgraded to commercial grade, with shiny, stainless steel appliances and gas-fueled ranges. The same giant table that sat twelve dominated the right side of the room, and Greta whisked and twirled from counter to table with a grace that spoke of years of practice.

She also appeared more at ease than he'd seen her in the last two days. The smile on her lips and the light in her eyes mesmerized him. Like a bloom on a cactus, she was the beauty on the prickly testosterone-laden men in her company.

Before he knew it, his feet moved him further into the room. All talking and the clank of utensils on dishware came to a halt as his presence was noticed. Mark sat at the table along with four other men who stopped, some in mid-bite, to stare at him.

Trey wasn't sure what was more disconcerting, the curious stares or the fact he only recognized one other man at the table.

"Good morning, Trey." Greta's greeting broke the silence. "Have a seat." She turned back to the counter and placed a third waffle on a plate.

"Morning," he murmured. He tilted his head from side to side, stretching the muscles in his neck to ease some of his tension, then took a seat at the head of the table. The effort to relax was more difficult to achieve than he thought with four pairs of eyes watching him as though he had mange.

"Trey, you remember Ben?" Mark indicated the man seated to Trey's left.

"Oh, yeah." Trey nodded at the big barrel-chested man, then shook his hand. "It's good to see a familiar face. Keeping us in line like always?"

"I do what I can. Plus, who could give up Greta's cooking?" His smile was friendly enough, but his dark eyes stared into Trey's, much the same as Greta's had the night before, searching for that elusive something.

Mark went around the table for the rest of the introductions, "This here is Jack, and Steven there is our college man."

Each man shook Trey's hand with a firm grip and an open curiosity that made him want to shout at the top of his lungs that it was really him.

A young man with skin so tan his blond hair appeared platinum-white held out his hand. "It's good to see you again, Mr. Armstrong."

Trey blinked in surprise. *Mr.* Armstrong? "Thanks, Adam. Hey, I remember you! You're little Adam Maguire."

Adam smiled a crooked grin and nodded. "Yes, sir. But I am twenty-two now. Can we drop the 'little'?"

"Sure, sure." Trey grew lightheaded with the exhilaration of a new memory. "What are you doing working here and not on your dad's ranch?"

He rubbed his chin. "He's got my five older brothers there to help. And I wanted to work someplace where I wasn't 'little' Adam Maguire."

"I can appreciate that." Trey looked around the table and laughed. "Adam, huh? Ben and Adam." He chuckled and slapped Mark on the arm. "That's pretty funny, huh, Hoss?"

Jack dropped his fork, the clatter echoing in the instantly

silent room. All eyes were on Trey as if he had suddenly sprouted a second head.

Maybe they weren't *Bonanza* fans. "What did I say?"

Steven was the first to recover. "Nothing, it's just…well, I've never heard you laugh before. Hell, I don't think I've ever seen you smile—Ow! Mark!" The young man backed away from the table and rubbed his shin.

"Coffee, Trey?" Greta placed a steaming mug of dark brew before him.

"Yeah, uh, sure." He eyed Steven with a circumspective stare. What the hell did that mean? Never smile? Him? That couldn't be right. His mother had often accused him of not being serious enough. He would have questioned it further, but everyone hunkered over their plates and shoveled food in like it was going to walk away.

Trey sat back and took a sip of coffee. It was good, but it burned like acid when it hit his belly. "Can I get some cream?"

Greta blinked at him with wide owlish eyes. "Cream?"

Why did she sound as if he was speaking another language? "Cream. For my coffee."

"Oh, of course. I'm sorry, you just usually drink it black."

"Is it bad that I want cream?" The high of experiencing an earlier memory crashed and burned with the reminder that his memory wasn't all back.

She gave a little laugh. "It's just cream, Trey. It's all right."

"How's the shoulder?" Mark asked around a mouthful of bacon.

"Fine. A bit sore. But good." Greta set a plate of waffles in front of him along with a bowl of slightly mashed blackberries. "Thanks, magpie. This looks great." She beamed at him before turning away. A second later she peeked over her shoulder and gave him another shy smile. A bolt of electricity raced up his spine, seeing the effect of his compliment.

With Greta's smile bolstering his spirits, he turned back to his breakfast and loaded his plate with toppings. The tender waffle melted in his mouth, the berries were sweetened to perfection, and the cream was whipped just right.

As Trey closed his eyes to fully appreciate the party in his mouth, Mark interrupted with a heavy sigh.

"Some coyotes dug under the fence and killed a calf last night. Colby is out in the field right now making sure there aren't any more. I wouldn't be concerned, except it's the second time this week." He paused when Greta set the carton of half-and-half in front of Trey.

She brushed a lock of hair from his forehead before walking around to take her seat at the other end of the table.

He tried really hard to concentrate on Mark and the discussion about the coyotes, but for the life of him, he could not tear his gaze away from his wife. She wore those jeans he was beginning to love, and a bright red T-shirt that clung in all of the right places.

Steven said something to her, and she laughed with a toss of her hair. The lyrical notes of her laughter hovered above the rumble of male voices in a soothing melody. The strained look she wore the day before was gone, and he hoped that he had something to do with that.

But the joy of her radiance was distorted at his end of the table by the impenetrable duo of Ben and Jack. Neither man said a word, but they watched him with brooding stares that made him feel as if he were being measured and weighed, and judgment about his worth had yet to be determined.

"What do you think, Hoss?"

"What?"

Mark smirked behind his mug. "What do you think about

nightly patrols around the perimeter until those coyotes are stopped?"

"Oh. Good. That sounds good." Trey bobbed his head as if he had been listening.

"Right." Mark's grin suggested he knew otherwise.

Adam stood and gathered his dishes. "Thank you, Miss Greta, that was excellent."

"Yes, ma'am," Steven agreed. "What's for dinner?" His eyes sparkled with the possibilities.

Greta smiled and her cheeks turned pink with all of the praise. "Lasagna."

"With garlic bread?"

"Of course."

All of the men moaned. Steven even rolled his eyes and wiped the imaginary drool from his mouth. Adam made a smart-ass comment about Jack's girlfriend being a vampire, which launched a volley of disparaging remarks about each other's women as they all helped clear the table.

Trey stood amid the teasing and camaraderie, painfully aware that he didn't belong. It was as if he was watching them from inside a bubble, present but not acknowledged. He didn't miss the way the men hovered around Greta, like worker bees protecting their queen, occasionally sneaking suspicious glances his way as if he was a threat to her well-being. Was their behavior because of his accident, or had he always on the outside looking in? Or worse?

"Hey." He spoke before he realized he formed the thought. "If it doesn't mess up anyone's plans, how about tomorrow night we have a cookout in the fire pit? We still have the fire pit, right?"

As one, the group turned to gape at him with their mouths open in shock. The silence was so deep, his own breathing sounded like a bull ready to charge. What the hell had he said now?

"That's a good idea, Hoss." Mark nodded. His approval spurred the group into action and murmurs of agreement. "We could do with a little fun and relaxation."

"I'll go to the market on my way back from the post office," Greta suggested with an overly bright smile. "And I'll have the butcher send over some steaks." She passed each man a huge metal lunchbox. "Here are your lunches. Be safe today."

One by one, they headed out until only Ben remained.

"How are you really doing?" he asked Trey in that deep bass voice that as a kid always made him snap to attention.

Apparently, the reaction continued into adulthood. He straightened his posture. "As well as can be, I guess. Greta's been a real help."

"You've got yourself a fine woman there. If nothing else, hold on to that." A meaty hand clapped Trey on his good shoulder. "I'll see you out on the field."

When they were finally alone, Trey turned to Greta. "What the hell did I say?'

"Hmm?" She barely glanced in his direction as she started placing plates in the dishwasher.

"Why did everyone stare at me like I was an alien? And what did Steven mean about me not smiling?" It didn't make sense. Was he not happy here?

"He was just exaggerating." She waved his concern away with a soapy hand. "You get pretty intense about the ranch. You expect a very high standard from all of the hands. I think... I think." She paused as if searching for the right words. "I think no one was expecting you to want to throw a party so soon after coming home."

Maybe she was right and he was reading too much into

things. Damn, he was getting paranoid. "I thought that maybe I would remember something if I got a chance to talk to everyone in a relaxed setting."

"It couldn't hurt." She closed the washer and set it to start. Her long dark hair fell down her back, kept off her face by a cheery red ribbon.

An image floated before his eyes of dark hair and a red ribbon lit by the light of the full moon. Greta smiling and laughing as she twirled in circles. He blinked several times, but the vision remained.

"Trey? Are you okay?" She took a step toward him as if he might fall over.

"Red ribbon," he whispered in voice that sounded low and distant.

"What?"

He pointed a shaky finger. "You wore a red ribbon in your hair the night we met."

Greta stilled, her lips parted. The blood rushed from her face, leaving her pale and trembling. Her mouth worked open and closed for several seconds before she spoke. "Yes. Yes, I did."

The cherrywood and stainless steel kitchen swam out of focus as he mentally fell back into the past.

Chapter 7

Seven years earlier...

THE NIGHT OF the Harvest Festival was unusually warm for October. Trey released the top button of his white Western-cut shirt in an attempt to get some relief from the stifling humidity. "Is it hot out?"

Mark, dressed similarly but all in black, looked at him in amusement. "Not especially. Is there a fire inside you that you can't put out?"

Trey rolled his eyes. "Funny."

Maybe Mark wasn't too far from the truth. No, there wasn't a fire, but there was definitely a need festering, an ache. Lately he'd been feeling a loneliness that went down to the soul. "Are you hooking up with Angela?"

Mark grunted. "No, we broke up a few weeks ago."

"Oh, sorry."

"No problem. Are you meeting Joanne?"

"Who?"

Mark laughed. "Joanne, the hairdresser."

"I haven't seen her in months." And even then it had been only the one date. It had taken all of five minutes for him to realize the bubbly blonde was not for him or his ranch.

"Really?" Their boots crunched along the gravel drive. "You know, Hoss, I think we've been working too hard. The ranch is doing well. The heifers are bred. Slaughtering is done for the season. I say let's kick back, drink some beers, kiss some girls, and have ourselves a right good time."

With Trey's golden-boy looks and Mark with his what the ladies called "smoldering darkness," they'd have no trouble procuring some female attention.

"Sounds good to me," Trey agreed. "And I'm Little Joe."

The entrance of the Martinez's orchard was already crowded as almost the entire town showed up for Mission's social event of the year. Although the trees were stripped of their fruit, the sweet smell of apples still hung in the air. A dance floor and boardwalk games were set up in the middle of the parking lot, complete with twinkle lights and bales of hay for decoration.

Trey's stomach rumbled as they passed the food stalls, but it wasn't food he hungered for. Mark was right. He had been working hard, really hard, and it was paying off. His parents' ranch was turning enough of a profit that he could start thinking about expanding and saving up for a new truck. Maybe even find a wife.

No, he wanted more than just a wife. What he longed for was a partner, a woman who'd work beside him, someone who sparked his interest all of the time and not only between the sheets. Unfortunately, he had yet to find the elusive soon-to-be Mrs. Armstrong. With him living in the middle of cattle country, most of the girls who hadn't gotten knocked up in high school had headed off to the big city to find adventure and men with money, leaving few prospects behind. Somehow, his future wife was going to have to drop into his lap, and he didn't think he was that fortunate.

Mark squeezed his way up to the makeshift bar and held up

two fingers. Within seconds he handed Trey an icy bottle.

He accepted it with a grateful nod, then took a big swig. His eyes prowled the crowded dance floor, noticing who had already hooked up and who stood in the shadows. He spotted Ben dancing with a pretty redhead. By the way the big man had her wrapped in his arms, Trey knew they weren't gonna stick around for long.

Joanne the hairdresser was there, and when their eyes met she huffed and turned her back on him. He lifted the bottle to his lips to hide his smile. Apparently, she was still smarting over being turned down for after-dinner entertainment.

"Hoss," he said to Mark, "I'm afraid it's going to be a long night."

As soon as the words left his mouth, the crowd on the dance floor parted, like a scene straight from the movies, and revealed the loveliest vision he'd ever seen.

A woman stood directly across the dance floor. Christmas lights hanging from up high picked up the red in her long dark hair, creating a seductive halo above her head like a neon sign flashing, "Here she is!" Holding that glorious mane in place was a fire-engine red ribbon that matched her silk dress, and her figure was straight out of 1950s Hollywood. Full breasts, a nipped-in waist that led to wide hips and shapely legs peeked out from under the hem of her flared skirt. She reminded him of a photograph of Jayne Mansfield his granddad used to have tacked up in his office in the barn and hidden from his grandmother.

Trey stared and stared until his eyes went dry and the bottle nearly slipped out of his fingers.

He glanced around the milling crowd to see who she was talking to and was surprised to see her with Mark's sister, Melody. Excellent, he had an in. His tongue worked overtime to get the moisture back in his mouth so he could speak.

"Hey, Hoss." He slapped Mark on the back. "Who's your sister talking to?"

Mark looked over his shoulder then froze. After a long lingering pause, his gaze slid back to Trey and proceeded to look him up and down. Heaving a big sigh, he muttered, "I should have known."

Hah, he did know her. "Who is she?"

Mark took his sweet time pulling a long draft from his bottle. The curve of his lips suggested he was enjoying making Trey wait. "Ah," he sighed after swallowing. "That was a mighty fine beer."

"Who is she?" Trey barely kept from growling.

"Her name is Greta. She's Melody's roommate's cousin. She's from over the mountains visiting for a while. I think she's teaching a course this quarter at the college."

"A course in what?"

Mark shrugged and began to peel the label off the bottle. "I don't remember. She's smart and seems nice."

"*Seems* nice? Have you met her?" He bit back a curse when Mark continued to look away. "Why didn't you tell me?"

Mark snorted and looked at him as if he had gone insane. "Tell you what? Melody's roommate's cousin's in town? Why would I tell you that?"

"Because she's the most beautiful woman in the world?"

Mark looked back over at Greta and kissed her curves with a scrutinizing gaze. "You think so?"

"Are you blind? Half the men here can't keep their eyes off her." Which was true, because he'd been taking note of which potential suitors he could take out if it came down to a fight.

Hold up. Trey knew Mark was a connoisseur of fine women. There was no way he would not find Greta attractive. Unless... "Have you asked her out?"

"What?" Mark shuffled from side to side.

"You did. You asked her out and she turned you down, didn't she?"

"Said something about cowboys and bad news," he mumbled as he looked at the ground.

"Introduce me."

"No."

"Come on. Introduce me." He grabbed Mark by the shirtfront and dragged him through the crowd.

"Damn it, Trey," Mark grumbled. "I can walk on my own." He knocked off Trey's grip and smoothed down the front of his shirt.

Trey's heart pounded a thundering beat as he drew closer. In a field of daisies, she was like an orchid, exotic and rare. He knew deep in his gut that in the next few seconds, his life was going to change forever.

"Ladies," Mark greeted as they approached. "Are you enjoying yourselves?"

"Checking up on me, big brother?" Melody pouted. "Hey, Trey," she said, with a flirtatious smile.

Mark's sister, and her roommate Gina, had been giving him the eye since they learned the difference between boys and girls. And Trey was always careful to never give the girls cause to act on that flirtation. Mostly because he never felt the same way back and second, Mark would have killed him.

"Melody, Gina," he said with a nod and turned to his dream woman. "Hi, I'm Trey Armstrong."

Eyes the color of the darkest chocolate looked up at him. The most luscious lips he had ever seen broke into a wide smile. "Hello." That one word came out so smoothed and cultured he felt it slide all the way down his spine. "I'm Gina's cousin, Greta O'Neal."

She held out her hand. Her palm was smooth, but small calluses roughened the pads of her fingers. He wondered what the difference in texture would feel like stroking over the rest of his body. His wild thoughts, however, were cut short by her very business-like handshake. For such a little thing, the firmness of her grip surprised him. Even in her three-inch heels, she barely reached his chin, but there was enough meat on her bones that he knew he could love her long into the night and she'd be able to take every thrust.

"How are you, Mark?" She offered a soft smile.

"Fine, thank you." He didn't quite meet her gaze. "You look beautiful." When his sister sulked, he quickly amended. "Oh yeah, you look nice too." Then he finally noticed Melody's plunging neckline. "What the hell are you wearing?"

Trey turned Greta away from the bickering brother and sister. "Dance with me, Greta."

She arched an amused eyebrow at his command. "Excuse me?"

"Come on. Dance with me." The request rolled off his tongue like a dare.

She looked him over with shrewd calculation in her eyes. Her gaze touched him from the top of his shaggy head to the bottom of his dusty boots and back up again. Did her breath catch when it passed over his belt buckle? 'Cause his sure did. It felt like an eternity passed until her weighted gaze returned to ensnare his as she slowly reached out and took his outstretched hand. His heart resumed its beating. He felt as if he'd been put to a test and passed.

The fates smiled upon him, and the band started to play a slow song when they stepped on to the dance floor. Her posture was perfect. Sophistication and class graced her every movement as her arms swung along her side. She was like Grace Kelly in his mom's favorite movie, *To Catch a Thief.*

Greta didn't protest when he wrapped his arms around her waist and pulled her in tighter than was proper for a first dance. Her arms encircled his neck and her hands rested along his nape. Greta's softness felt so good against him, his body grew hard and his blood heated. He shuddered and felt the sweat gather along his spine.

She was in his arms, like he wanted. Now what?

"So, Greta, where are you from?" Damn. That was original.

"Seattle."

When she didn't elaborate, his mind went blank. Usually, every woman he was with loved to talk about themselves. Never before had it been up to him to fill the silence.

"How long are you visiting for?"

"Until the end of November. I'm teaching a class at Central this quarter."

"You're a teacher?"

"Not really." The corner of her lip quirked up. "I'm more of an artist."

"An artist?" He said the word as if he'd never heard it before.

"Yes. I make jewelry. I'm teaching a class on jewelry making."

His forehead puckered. "They teach that in college?"

She laughed at his confused expression. "Yes, they do."

"Wow. I've never met an artist before."

"I never would have guessed." Sarcasm dripped from her words.

"Can you actually earn a living at being an artist?" So what if he sounded a bit like a hick. In his world, practicality meant the difference between making profit or losing his shorts.

"Yes," she said on another laugh. "Can you make a living at

ranching?"

"I sure am trying. Hey, how do you know I'm a rancher?"

"You're Mark's boss. I've heard of you."

"Really?" He gave her his best bad-boy smile. "What have you heard?"

Her answering smile was just as wicked. "That you're a rancher."

"And?"

"That's all." She shrugged. The teasing light in her eyes made him wonder if she was playing with him.

"Hmm. Did you hear I could dance?" Before she could answer, he twirled her out, then in, her skirt flaring in an elegant arc around her knees. Then he spun them in a circle and finished in a low dip. Both of them were panting a bit heavier as he drew her back upright.

Her eyes sparkled as she looked him over again, this time visibly impressed. "Very smooth."

"Thank you." He smiled smugly. "Have dinner with me."

Her smooth brow crinkled even as her lips curled up. "Demanding thing, aren't you?"

"Only when it comes to something I want. Go out with me. Please?" he added for good measure.

She batted her long lashes batted up at him. "Thank you, but no."

"No?" Damn, he thought he had her. "Why not?"

"I don't think it would be a good idea."

"I heard you told Mark that cowboys were bad news."

Greta looked away, slightly chagrined. "Maybe."

"And you would know that how?" Had she had a bad experience with a past boyfriend? The thought of her with another man made his grip tighten around her waist.

"I just do," she said in all seriousness. "I'm not the kind of woman you're looking for."

He raised his own brow at that. "What kind am I looking for?"

"You small-town boys are all the same. The long-term plan is to find a good little wife who will keep the home fires burning. One you can keep barefoot in the kitchen and popping out your babies whenever you choose. But for tonight, you're looking for an easy lay. And I'm neither one of those."

"Now, darling, that hurts. It's not fair to judge me so."

"Tell me that was not your plan when you came here tonight."

She had him there on both fronts. Holding her this close, it was all too easy to imagine waking up beside her every morning. Starting a family, building a future. Apparently his expression showed his thoughts, because she stiffened and pulled away.

"No, no, hold on. Hold on." He herded her like a wayward steer. "You've known me for all of two seconds, and you have our future already laid out. Let's take it one day at a time."

"Look," she said sharply. "I'm only here for a few months, and I don't do short term."

"It's just one date," he coaxed.

"You'll break my heart." Her soft words barely reached his ears.

"Why would you say that?" he asked just as quietly.

"Guys like you don't know how to treat girls like me. It's inevitable."

At some point they had stopped dancing, and she stood cradled in his arms. "I'd never hurt you, Greta."

She sniffed in disbelief. "You don't know that."

"Yes, I do." He leaned closer until a whisper separated them. Holding her there, gazing into her rich brown eyes, he was never more certain of anything in his life. "Deep down, in my gut, I know that I could never hurt you."

Greta looked away, her lips pinched tight. A fine tremble shook her shoulders. This sudden glimpse of her vulnerability drew him in like bees to sweet nectar.

He couldn't resist the temptation to taste her. He tracked light kisses across her cheek to her ear. Ruby red drops hung from her earlobes and sparkled against the pale flesh. Her skin was so soft under his lips. Another shudder coursed through her body.

"Twirl me," she said suddenly.

"What?" Her words were slow to penetrate to his brain.

"Spin me out."

Trey was willing to give her anything she asked. With a grace even he didn't know he possessed, he spun her away from him, then back in. He twirled her away one more time and she let go. In a blink, she was gone.

Trey frantically searched for her in the crowd, jumping up and down like on a pogo stick, trying try to catch a glimpse. In a sea of gingham, he spotted her red dress waving at him like a flag to a bull. He charged after her, nostrils flaring. He wasn't deterred yet.

She wasn't running away from him, she was running from herself. For a smart woman, Greta was acting like a scared little girl. She wanted him, she didn't think she did, but Trey sensed her desire, and he was not going to let her walk away without giving him a chance.

His long legs quickly ate up what little distance she placed between them. "Don't run," he said as he caught her by the elbow and turned her around.

Fire burned in her eyes. "Don't play me for a fool. You were trying to *claim* me in front of everyone. What, you kiss a woman on the dance floor at the country bumpkin festival and she's tied to you forever?"

Trey ran an agitated hand through his hair. "Jesus, woman, you drive me crazy. I like you, and I want to know more about you. You, you—aw, hell." He scooped her close and crushed his lips to hers.

His mouth devoured hers, his tongue plundered. Her body melted against him while his hardened, every muscle growing tight and achy.

When Trey pulled away, he knew he had branded her as his, just as surely as if he had used a hot iron.

Greta blinked up at him, dazed. Her lips parted, the plump little pillows swollen and wet as she tried to smooth out her breathing. The fact he was the one to cause that reaction made him want to bay at the moon. He waited with a patience bred from confidence for her to beg him to take her some place private and properly claim her as his.

A light sparked in her eyes as those juicy lips curved into a smile. Then she laughed.

And kept on laughing.

The tinkling notes rose in the air and danced with the rustling of the trees. She leaned back, one hand at her throat, the other on her belly, while Trey continued to stare at her in confusion.

"What?"

"I'm sorry," she gasped as she struggled to regain her composure. She wiped away a tear, smudging her eyeliner. "I just wasn't expecting that. Do you practice kissing on those cows of yours?"

Was that an insult? "What do you mean?"

Another giggled escaped. "I find it funny that 'Love-'em-and-leave-'em' Trey Armstrong is a piss-poor kisser."

"Piss—" Oh, now he didn't know if he wanted to strangle

her or take her against the tree just to make her eat her words. "Not so loud, woman." He took a menacing step closer. "What are you talking about? I've never had any complaints before."

"Maybe they didn't know any different." She smirked. "You're so big and muscle-ly, and hard." Her eyes burned a trail over his frame, and he saw her suppress a tremble. She blinked and came back from whatever world she went to. "But your kiss was soft, and squishy, and *wet*. You're a sloppy kisser, Trey." She shook her head, the ends of her dark hair swinging around her shoulders like a cape.

"You think you can do better?"

A dainty hand settled on her hip. "Oh, honey, I know I can."

"Prove it." His tone was low and dangerous. "Or are you scared?"

The dare hung in the air between them. If she took it, he'd see to it that they both won. But if she ran, they'd both lose.

Thank his lucky stars, she took the bait. Stepping right up to him, she grazed her breasts against his chest as she tilted her chin up. He sucked in a breath and waited for her next move. It was up to her to prove him wrong.

She gazed into his eyes, hypnotizing him with their smoky intent. "Don't move," she whispered. Her lips brushed his when she spoke.

Slower than a spring thaw, she pressed her mouth to his in a brief touch. Then she pulled back and tilted her head to fit them perfectly together. Her full lips were surprisingly firm as they massaged his. She didn't take, she didn't give. She exchanged pleasure.

Trey stood there helpless, hands limp at his sides, his mind focused on nothing but her texture. Her petal-soft lips eased his open and he wallowed in her mulberry wine flavor. The delicate slide of her tongue glided along his bottom lip before dipping in to tease. She tasted exotic and forbidden.

Her hands gripped the sides of his belt to bring them flush together. His cock grew thick and hard behind the confines of his jeans until the throbbing grew painful. He ground his hips into her, trying to find relief, but all it did was fan his passion.

Greta pulled back to look at him through heavy-lidded eyes. All he could do was stand there as his lungs struggled for air. His entire world consisted only of Greta.

Those fantastic lips, now void of all lipstick, curled into a grin and brushed against his once more.

"See you around, cowboy."

Then she turned and strode away as if they were two strangers on the street exchanging nothing more than a polite nod in passing.

Trey watched her go, her hips rolling under her skirt in an easy glide that said she was in charge of her world. His hand went to adjust his belt buckle and relieve the pressure in his balls that were near to bursting as his lips still tingled.

Despite his discomfort, he smiled.

"Oh, it's on, Miss Greta O'Neal. You're mine."

"THE HARVEST FESTIVAL. You wore a red dress," Trey rasped as the kitchen came back into focus.

"Yes." Greta exhaled, as if she had been holding her breath the entire time he'd been remembering. "Is it all back? Do you remember?" Her entire body was taut, vibrating with expectancy.

"No," he drew out slowly. "I remember meeting you. Dancing. Kissing." He chuckled. "That kiss was something else. You were right. I was a horrible kisser." She swayed, her posture relaxing as she smiled with him. "And then you left me there, aching and lonely."

"You didn't stay away for too long."

"How long after that were we married?"

A blush rose on her pale skin. "Six months."

Trey laughed at that. "What changed your mind about me?"

Greta eased back against the counter and batted her lashes. "Besides your charm?" she teased. "It was your persistence and willingness to learn."

"No, really. What changed your mind?" The need to know the answer seemed vitally important. He didn't know why, it just did.

"Well." She bit her lip as she thought. He liked that she considered her words before she spoke. "It was your persistence and willingness to learn. I'm serious. You listened to me. You let me, encouraged me, to be me. You never asked me to be anyone else. That's a very attractive trait."

All teasing aside, the sincere light in her eyes and soft smile told him she meant every word. He leaned closer and braced his hands on the counter, trapping her in the circle of his arms. "You were the prettiest thing I had ever seen." He lifted his hand to brush his thumb across her cheek. "You still are."

With a small sigh, she glanced at the floor. Greta was every bit as breathtaking now as she had been then. But now it was different. Where was that fireball who had tempted and drove him crazy with her obstinacy? The woman before him was delicate, almost fragile in her beauty. Strain that had nothing to do with age lined her face.

What had happened to Greta, to him? Trey couldn't discount what his men had said earlier about his lack of humor, or the older man he had seen in the mirror the day before. Had it been the death of their son that caused the change? The death of a child would take its pound of flesh. Or was there more to their story?

"I guess I'm not so much of a stranger now," she joked with a slight tremor in her voice.

He cupped her face in his palms. "You've never been a stranger to me, Greta. I told you before. My head might not remember, but my body does. My heart does."

Apprehension clouded her expression. The knowledge that he did something to instill this distrust ate at him.

Anxious to prove he spoke the truth, he pressed his lips to hers. Just a touch. No asking, no demanding, just being. For several long seconds, he enjoyed the feel of her in his arms. This was a promise. His vow to protect her, to honor and to cherish her. Somehow, some way, he was going to right whatever wrong he had done.

Of course, if he knew what that was, his task would be that much easier. But Greta was a proud woman. He was going to have to figure out this mystery on his own.

Trey looked down at his wife and felt the first real assurance that this was where he belonged. He remembered her. Not a dream or thought implanted by someone else's stories. He actually had a memory of her that he could claim as his own.

Greta slid her small hands around his waist and held him tight. Trey sighed, his breath ruffling her hair.

He remembered.

Chapter 8

TREY BURIED HIS nose into Greta's hair for one last inhale of her fresh scent before reluctantly drawing out of her embrace. "You make it difficult to think of work."

"You're not going out in the field, are you? Trey, you're supposed to rest." The cutest crinkle formed between her brows as her fingers curled into his shirt.

He dropped a kiss on her forehead and rubbed her tense shoulders. "I'm not gonna take on too much, but I am the boss. I still have to pull my weight."

Her soft breasts pressed into his chest, drawing his attention to the deep cleavage. "Why don't you come with me into town? We could stop by the bakery, pick up a slice of your favorite cheesecake, and have a picnic along the river." She looked up at him, her eyes big with a promise of something sweeter than pastry. "Maybe we can spark some memories together."

A groan welled up from his throat before he could stop himself. "Lord almighty, woman. How did I ever make this ranch a success with you tempting me with every breath?"

A dimple appeared with her grin. "I told you, you're very driven when you're going after something you want."

"Right now, I want this." He gathered the hair at her nape in his fist to hold her still for his kiss.

Not that she protested his fierce possession. Greta allowed him in with a sigh, her tongue tangling with his. She tasted sweeter than the berries he had for breakfast and was so intoxicating he swayed on his feet, lost to the fiery woman who burned in his arms. Her whimpers grew louder with each pass of his hands along the curve of her hip, the small of her back, and around to palm her full breast. Her nipple poked through the cotton to scrape against his palm with an enticing rasp. He backed her up against the counter, grinding his shaft into the softness of her belly.

Had they done this before? How many times had they stolen a moment and made mad crazy love on that big kitchen table? Did he ever paint her bouncing breasts with maple syrup and lick her clean as he pounded them both to oblivion? Well, he was going to soon, if he had any say in the matter. Screw work and reacquainting himself with his life. All he needed was right there between his wife's thighs.

He cupped her ass, giving a squeeze before lifting her up. White-hot pain lanced across his shoulder and down his arm.

"Fuck," he groaned and jumped back so fast he stumbled on his feet. "Sorry, sorry. Guess I'm not quite ready for strenuous activity."

"Are you all right?" Greta whispered through swollen lips. A pink flush graced her cheeks, and she sagged against the Sub-Zero refrigerator at her side.

"I'm fine. Just…" he struggled to catch his breath. "Completely out of my head."

What the hell happened? He had a plan—explore the ranch, examine his surroundings, and regain his memory. Added to that stress was the fact that a few of his men didn't seem to have the best opinion of him. Getting caught fucking in the kitchen while they were working his land was not going to improve that impression. He needed space. A couple hundred acres of space to reset his priorities.

"Go," he said as he took two steps back. None of his blood was feeding his big brain and forming a sentence was near to impossible. "Nothing will get done if we stay in touching distance. That's probably a bad idea, though I can't think of why right now."

She nodded but continued to stare up at him with those big doe eyes sparkling with desire.

"Later. I promise." He stumbled into the humid outdoors and made his way across the driveway to the barn. The sticky heat did nothing to cool his libido.

Man, it was going to be a long day.

The thought made him smile. Torture had never been sweeter.

Sunshine spilled through the entrance of the stable, leaving the rest of the barn in shadows. He waited a second for his eyes adjust to the change in light before strolling down the main aisle and stopping at the second stall from the end.

At over fifteen hands high with golden skin and a pale yellow mane, the quarter horse was already standing by the door waiting for him.

"So, you're Lucky." Trey reached out to the stallion. His fingers gently traced the white star on his forehead. "Do I even want to know what happened to Chance?"

There would only be one reason why his favorite horse was not around. Trey closed his eyes with a sigh. Did everything around him die? Yes, he lived on a ranch and he knew all about the circle of life, but damn. How much loss could one man have in his lifetime?

Lucky seemed to sense his heavy heart and butted his nose

against Trey's chest.

Trey rested his cheek alongside Lucky's neck. "Can you tell me what happened a few days ago? I've been riding horses my whole life. Did I fall off?"

He inhaled deep and the scent of horse and hay filled his nostrils. In his mind he imagined it was the day of his accident, he was back on the horse, riding through the field. Scenario after scenario of how he might have become injured flitted behind his closed eyelids. Had Lucky gotten spooked? Had he not paid attention? A fall off the saddle did not seem capable of causing so much damage.

When his head hurt from thinking so hard, he gave the horse one last pat. "We won't be going riding for a few days, but I'll take you out later to get some sunshine."

Toward the back of the barn in what used to be the tack room was his office. At least that was where it was located now. When he was younger, the office had always been in the main house in the den, filled with his grandfather's hunting trophies and mother's photo albums. For the life of him, he couldn't remember when the move to the barn had been made or why, but he knew this location was where he did all of the bookwork for the ranch.

The office door opened on well-oiled hinges. Two tiny windows on either side of the room let in some light, but it was still dim in a dark, scary movie kind of way. A flip of the switch turned on the desk lamp.

He looked around, stupefied. "Are you kidding me?"

The desk was what he expected, as were the filing cabinets, but not the overwhelming stockpiles of books. Whatever wall space was available was taken up by floor to ceiling bookcases. Each shelf was filled with neat stacks of hardcover and paperback books, with more piled on the floor.

"These can't be mine," he murmured as he twirled in circles and scratched his head.

Between the ranch and his family, where would he have found the time to read all of them? Agriculture, science fiction, mystery. He didn't read science fiction. Did he?

"Why is it that the more I try to remember, the weirder things get?" He stepped over a set of weights and a medicine ball to get to the desk.

Behind the desk sat a wobbly, leather office chair that had seen better days. Stuffing spilled from the cracks in the fabric around the arms, and the wheels were missing from the metal legs. He slowly eased onto the seat and hoped the chair was strong enough to hold his weight. To his relief, the dark leather molded to his body as if it were made specifically for his ass.

On the scarred surface of the desk sat a desktop computer and several bins of paper stacked neatly with a profusion of colorful Post-it notes sticking out the side like a rainbow.

He opened a drawer and found more file folders, with payables and insurance information listed alphabetically with neat little labels affixed in the corners.

"Huh," he murmured and shut the drawer with a frown.

Mark must be the one doing the paperwork, since organization was not one of Trey's strong suits. Then again, it wasn't one of Mark's, either. At least it hadn't been. Trey never had the patience to maintain such immaculate files, preferring to be outside working the herd over dealing with numbers. He had counted it a success when he managed to enter the numbers on the correct spreadsheet on a somewhat timely basis. His accountant had required many a bribe to continue taking him as a client.

He turned attention to the computer and rapped his thumbs on the ink blotter while the machine hummed and booted up. Once it was on, Trey frowned in disbelief at the sheer number of folders spread out on the monitor's desktop. There were files and spreadsheets labeled with every aspect of the farm. Projections, actuals, breed versus feed ratios. He slumped in his chair as the number of man-hours it must have taken to create and populate all of those files boggled his mind.

What do I do next? He randomly clicked and dragged the mouse across the screen. Page after page opened up like a deck of cards shooting out of a magician's sleeve. *Ding-ding!* Error message. *What the hell?*

He pushed away from the computer as if the damn machine was set to explode any moment.

Unbelievable. He actually forgot how to use the computer. A chuckle started low in his belly then got caught in his throat. This might not be a good sign. With one last cautious glance at the frozen monitor, he got up and began to rummage through the rest of the office.

Two filing cabinets, three drawers high, contained more alphabetized and color-coded papers on every bull and heifer bought and sold on the ranch over the last seven years. The files were so well organized he wondered why the hell he needed the computer in the first place.

The bottom drawer on the last cabinet was locked. He took the keys off his belt loop and found the one with the same letter etched into the metal as the label on the cabinet. The drawer clicked opened without a hitch. Inside were payroll records, tax forms, and a large lockbox. The gray metal box was cold in his hands when he lifted it out.

He flipped the latch and raised the lid. A framed black and white photo of Greta's smiling face looked up at him. A river ran in the background behind her in the shot, and her shoulders were bare but for the straps of a bathing suit. Pure joy radiated from her eyes and wide grin. Serene, glowing, her alluring beauty took his breath away.

Underneath that frame was a second photo, this one a full color snapshot of the two of them taken in front of the house. In it they were hugging, and Greta had turned to face the camera. He looked so young, so happy. The both did. The man in the photo had a perfect world in his hands and knew it. This was the man Trey had expected to see in the mirror yesterday morning. God, had he aged.

The photo in last frame stopped his heart. The glass was smudged, as if it had been touched often. Trey added a few more prints as he ran his finger over the laughing faces. In a series of three photos, Trey and Greta were walking in a field. Between them was a tiny, dark-haired boy. In each succeeding image they had swung him higher and higher. Little Luke had had his father's eyes and his mother's dark hair. They had been a beautiful family.

Trey wasn't sure how long he sat crouched on the floor staring at that photo, but his joints popped when he finally stood, with the frame held firmly in his grip. How could he have forgotten them? Why were these photos locked in a box and not displayed on his desk with pride? Now that he thought about it, he didn't remember seeing any photos in the house, either.

None of this was making any sense. The house felt impersonal, while the office just creeped him out. No mementos anywhere. This was not the way he had pictured how his life would be.

Laughter, love, infinite possibilities. That was what was supposed to be in his future. This—he looked around the room and felt sick. This was the existence of a hermit, and he didn't like it one bit.

Well, if there was one thing he remembered he had always

believed in, it was that he was capable of learning new tricks.

With the decision made, he closed the lockbox with a snap. He strode to the desk and set the photos in positions of prominence. All that was important in life was right there. The people you loved and who loved you back. Never should they be hidden.

"Hey, Hoss, how're you doing?"

Trey glanced up at his childhood friend with trouble swirling in his gut. Mark watched him with that cool as a cucumber look he always wore. "Fine. I think." He rubbed his hand over his face. "I don't know. When did I move my office in here?"

Mark scratched his cheek as he thought back. "A year or so ago."

"Why?"

"Don't know."

Mark had a great poker face, but Trey had a suspicion that he did know. "It...man, it really doesn't feel like me." He squinted as he glanced around the dim interior. "It's so organized. Is this your work or Greta's?"

"Neither. You've been doing it all by yourself. I muddled through it when you were in the hospital. You have a lot of files on your desktop."

"Yeah." Trey laughed without humor. "I don't remember how to work it."

Mark frowned. "Work what?"

"The computer." He pointed to the frozen screen. "I broke it."

Mark stepped around the desk and reached for the mouse. A few clicks later he glanced sideways at Trey. "Damn, boy. That's funny," he said, laughing. Actually, it was more like a wheeze. Mark had a really dry sense of humor. "You really don't remember how to use the computer."

The corner of Trey's mouth lifted in chagrin. "I turned it on. I knew to point and click, but that's about all."

Mark punched a few keys, and the monitor went dark. "Maybe there's a manual around here."

Trey gestured to the stacks of novels piled in the corners. "Mark, whose books are these?"

He received an "Are you joking?" glance in response. "I would guess that they're yours, since you're the only one who comes in here."

That knowledge wasn't comforting. "What happened to me, Mark?"

Duh, his friend's raised eyebrows said. "You had an accident and lost your memory."

"Don't bullshit me." Why did it feel as if no one ever gave him a straight answer? "What happened to me before that? Whose room is this, really, because it can't be mine." With a snap of his wrist, he pulled out a file from a drawer and threw it on the desk. "Who color coordinates which brand of feed fed which set of cattle in a specific area of the pasture? There are books coming out of my ass. There are instruction manuals on Chevys here, Mark. Goddamn Chevys. What kind of a sick, twisted person lives here?"

Mark swallowed hard and looked away. Either he was trying not to laugh in Trey's face, or he found him so pathetic he couldn't look him in the eye.

"Look." He crossed his arms. "Luke's death affected all of us. You took it hard, and rightly so. Afterward," he paused to exhale in a loud rush. "Afterward, you kind of distanced yourself from everyone."

Distanced? Trey looked around the dark, cramped room. This wasn't distance. This was enforced solitude. Did he spend every waking hour in here? A thought hit him so hard, he felt it in his solar plexus. "Greta. What about Greta?"

Mark's jaw tightened, his gaze steady. "From everyone."

Trey sank slowly into the chair, which again molded to his ass like a second skin. He jumped to his feet as the truth set in. All of this craziness made sense now. He'd been hiding.

"Why didn't she tell me?"

"Maybe she didn't want you to remember the bad times." By the tone of his voice, Trey guessed they had been pretty bad.

Instantly, the room started to suffocate him. The shuttered windows, the dark furniture all seemed to close in around him like a straitjacket. "I-uh-I gotta get some air," he mumbled before escaping into the stable. Once he reached Lucky's stall, he reached for the nearest bridle and slipped it over the horse's head.

"I'll close up here for you," Mark said from the door, but Trey was already mentally gone.

In the bright sunshine, he was finally able to draw a decent breath. This was where he belonged. Out in the sunlight, not in some cave plotting the location of each blade of grass. It just didn't seem plausible that Luke's death affected him so deeply that hiding was preferable to being with loved ones. His mom and dad had been everything to him. They taught him the importance of family, and he couldn't believe that he would give up on Greta and his friends.

Greta.

Now he understood her hesitation and lack of trust he had been sensing. She was expecting him to push her away again. Burned once, Greta was probably protecting herself from any more future heartache. Somehow he was going to have to find a way to convince her that he wanted to start over. The past was the past and couldn't be changed. The only direction for them to go was forward.

Hours later and he was still processing what he had learned. Several times he was tempted to search for Greta and confront her with his newly gained knowledge, but then he'd chicken out and scoot back into the safety of the sun, even going so far as to sneak a sandwich out of the kitchen when his belly rumbled instead of asking her for assistance.

The subject of his mental desertion needed to be broached delicately, if he even wanted to go there at all. The fact that Greta hadn't done more than wave at him from a window or the porch with that anxious furrow on her brow was just as telling.

As the sun started its descent, the dinner bell rang. A call to come home. He led Lucky back to his stall, his gaze landing on the door to the office. The coldness of the cave, or the warmth of the house?

There really was no competition.

MARK WAS ALREADY in the mudroom when Trey entered. "How are you doing, Hoss?"

"I'm going to be just fine." He met his friend's gaze head on, determined to tread a new path.

Mark nodded then finished washing up. When they entered the dining room together, Colby and Jack were already seated at the table.

"Whoa," Steven exclaimed as he took a seat at the head of the table. "I didn't expect to see you here, boss man."

Trey stiffened. "Let me guess. You don't see me much at supper either?"

"Nope." He laughed. "Until breakfast, I don't think I've ever seen you eat at all. We all joke that you eat nothing but dust and paper." He laughed again.

That hyena cackle made Trey's palm itch to pop him one on

the back of the head. "Well, I'm starving, and Greta's a fantastic cook. It's one of the many reasons why I married her."

Greta fumbled the heavy tray of lasagna that she was placing on the table and looked at him in surprise.

"Did you get your memory back?" Jack asked. Several pairs of eyes turned to Trey in expectation.

"It's coming back slowly. But so far, it's been good." He didn't want to let on just how much he had remembered, or at least, what he had figured out. Greta obviously didn't want to bring up his self-imposed imprisonment, and he didn't want her to worry about him returning to that solitude. He was done running, and he was ready to reassure her of that just as soon as he got her alone. His cock stirred as he thought about the way he planned on doing the convincing.

All through dinner he watched his wife, caressing her with a heat in his gaze that made her flush and her chest rise and fall with a rapid breath. He wanted to let loose with a big goofy grin seeing the effect he had on her. The bold, brash Greta, who seared his soul with one kiss the night they met, would not have blushed with such shyness. After the fifth time she caught his eye, a slow smile curled up one corner of her mouth and she shook her head at him as if he were a scoundrel. Oh yeah, she read him correctly and did not seem opposed to his attention.

The conversation around him was just background noise as he kept his focus on his wife. The way she drank her wine, her smile, how she looked a person right in the eye when she spoke to them.

He felt his bemused grin turn into a frown as he watched her talk to Adam about a necklace she was making for him to give to his mother and he realized how far away from each other they sat. Why was he at the opposite end of the table from his woman? He wanted to be the one to sit next to her, ask her about her day while he held her hand. That was one more thing to add to his list of changes.

Dinner seemed to drag on forever and he nearly wept for joy when Greta started to stack dishes. "Would anyone like thirds or fourths?"

"I couldn't eat another bite. Right, fellas?" His tone left no room for argument.

After the men exchanged curious glances, general rumbles of consent followed.

Trey came around and took the plates from her hands. "We got this. Why don't you head on up and relax in a nice bath?" His gaze swept up and down her body as if he were imagining being in the tub with her.

Greta's breathing hitched. "Are you sure?"

"Oh yeah, magpie, I'm sure." Lust and desire roughened his voice.

"Okay." She walked toward the doorway, only to pause. Lip between her teeth, she glanced back at him as if to reassure herself that she had understood him correctly.

He put all of the want and need he felt for her in his eyes and the predatory curl of his grin. In response, that siren's smile, the one he fell in love with when they first met, flitted across her lips before she turned and walked away.

Trey anticipated cleanup to take only a few minutes with the extra hands, and he rushed to the kitchen to do his share.

"Man, can you imagine Greta in the bathtub?" Steven was saying as he entered. "Do you think she uses bubbles or that bath oil stuff? I would love to see her all slippery." He turned to throw away the paper towel he was using to wipe down the counter and froze when he saw Trey. "Uh, not that I ever imagine Greta naked, or clothed. I don't think of her at all," he added hastily. The flush that raced up his neck brought out the freckles in his cheeks.

Trey arched a brow and placed the dishes in the sink. "Do you often talk about my wife in such a manner?"

The room went deathly quiet as everyone watched Steven pale. His throat worked up and down as he swallowed. Was he rethinking that third helping of lasagna? "No, sir. I wouldn't do that."

"And why not?" he asked, low and dangerous.

"Because it's disrespectful, and we shouldn't covet our boss's anything."

Trey nodded. "That's right." He took a quick glance around. "I think you can handle the rest, right, Steven? I'm gonna see if my wife needs help with her bath."

Cat calls and whistles echoed behind him as he made his way up the stairs with an anticipatory smile.

Chapter 9

T HE BATHROOM DOOR was open a hair, which Trey took as an invitation to enter. On silent feet, he crept into the steamy oasis and stopped dead in his tracks.

Greta was reclining in the tub. Hair up, eyes closed, she was the poster girl for relaxation. With the clear water, he had an unimpeded view of her curvy body. One leg was bent with her knee guarding her womanly secrets. Cinnamon-colored nipples barely broke through the water's surface and glistened with temptation. Man, he couldn't wait to taste them.

He should have taken her that morning. To deny himself something he wanted so badly that his teeth and balls ached had been the most boneheaded promise he ever made, especially when she was his for the taking. But no, he had to be an honorable bastard.

And now the possibilities flipping through his head as quickly as a teenager with a remote control were not in the least bit honorable.

"No bubbles?" he asked. Desire made his voice raspy.

She jerked in surprise, causing a little splash before she slowly rolled her head in his direction. She lifted her lashes. "That was quite the ninja move there. I didn't even hear your boots on the tile."

"No bubbles?" he repeated, lost to all but her.

She caught her plump lower lip between her teeth, stifling her grin. "Earlier, I was getting the impression that you might be planning on kissing me all over."

Despite her bold words, he saw her slight tremble and the uncertainty in her gaze. She was bracing herself as if she expected him to reject her. No way in hell was that going to happen.

"That would be correct," he said.

Her tongue flicked out and wet her lips. His words must have pleased her, for she glowed with an inner light that tempted and beckoned. "If that was true, then I wanted you to taste my skin, and not bath soap."

Geez-us. He had his boots off in seconds, followed by his belt that hit the floor with a clang. "Stand up," he commanded.

Like a goddess from the deep, Greta rose from the water. Glistening and ripe, she was ready to be plucked. Trey grabbed the nearest towel and began to dry her pink skin. He hunkered down on one knee to pay special attention to her legs. With her delicate foot in his hand, he was right at eye level with the lips of her sex that were glistening wet, and not solely by bath water. The sight of her arousal snapped what little control he clung onto.

With a barely restrained growl, he threw the towel to the side and stood. The clip in her hair snapped in his hand as he whipped it out and tossed it over his shoulder, where it bounced off the mirror and clattered into the sink.

He dug his hands into her thick tresses and held her still while he ravaged her mouth. She softened against him, feeding his hunger with her submission. He supped on her lips until the pressure in his cock became too much to bear and he had to break away, sweeping her up in his arms.

"Trey, your arm," she protested even as she clung to his shoulders.

"Don't worry about me, magpie. I'm more than healthy enough to love you right."

He set her down on the bed like a precious treasurer. She rested back on her hands and watched him with her plump lower lip trapped between her teeth. Her bent knees gently bounced open and shut, teasing him with a glimpse of heaven. Dusty nipples peeked out from the long, dark hair covering her breasts.

"God, you're the sexiest thing I've ever seen," he rasped. Just looking at her made his hands shake. Greta's gaze never left him while he fumbled with the buttons on his shirt and wrestled the damn thing off his back. Her little pink tongue ran across her lips again. "Baby doll, I can't think when you look at me like that."

She husked out a wicked laugh as she watched him struggle with his zipper. The sound of the *tick-tick-tick* of the teeth as they released made his skin tighten around his flexing muscles. Once free from the constricting denim, he kicked off his jeans then crawled up her body.

The first brush of skin on skin made them both hiss in pleasure. Bracing himself on his good arm, Trey trailed his other hand down the smooth column of her throat then over her full breast. Her nipple beaded at his touch, begging for attention. It took all of his restraint to not fall all over her like a dog with a bone.

Greta arched her back when he took the hardened tip between his lips. With each pull of his mouth, her head thrashed back and forth on her pillow. He loved the way her hair billowed in a wild cloud around her. Her skin flushed a pretty pink in a visual thermometer of her arousal as he lashed the other peak with the tip of his tongue. Her hips moved against him, telling him where she wanted his touch the most.

He pressed soft kisses down her sternum and across her ribs. In the lamplight's soft glow, silvery tracks crossed her belly, a physical reminder that she had carried their child. Not only had she carried him, but she had loved him with all of her heart and soul. A gift like that needed to be honored.

With his lips and tongue, he traced every line, worshipped every inch while her fingers cradled his head and massaged his scalp.

"Oh, Trey," she sighed so softly, he almost missed the longing, the sound of reclaiming what once was lost, in her whisper. Almost.

With his callused hand, he smoothed the inside of her quivering thigh and found her wet and open for him. He pushed a thick finger inside, muscles suckling on the digit in greedy draws.

Damn, she was tight. He worked in a second finger to stretch and prepare her for his possession.

"I need to taste you, baby," he mumbled as he shouldered her thighs further apart.

He placed his mouth against her liquid center and began to lick and suck on her little pearl. Her hips bucked and jerked in his grip. It seemed as if she couldn't decide if she wanted to press closer or pull away. He loved the power he had over her writhing body. There was no second guessing there. No uncertainty. Instinctually he knew exactly how to please this woman. His heart filled with the knowledge that he could provide this for her all on his own.

Greta's low and throaty sighs drove him to distraction. Occasionally, a deep, sexy moan escaped her lips, but otherwise she communicated all of her pleasure with breathy pants and the roll of her hips. The sound poured over him like warm honey, stroking him like a physical caress that made his body ache and his cock harder. He was so ready, cum dripped from the tip. Man, he wanted her now, but he needed to see her pushed to beyond all reason first.

"Please, Trey, please. I need you inside me," she panted, tugging on his hair.

A third finger pushed deep. "Doesn't this feel good?"

She actually had the temerity to glare down at him through her pleasure. "It's fantastic, but I want you. I need your cock inside me. Deep."

The cock in question jerked, pleased to be called upon. "Soon. Give me what I want, then I'll give you what you want."

She fell back with a groan that made him smile in triumph. He took her clit into his mouth again, and sucked hard as his fingers played her like a fine instrument. Seconds later she broke, bucking in his hold and filling his mouth with her sweet cream as he moaned through the orgasm with her. His eyes watered as she pulled on his hair, but he didn't mind one bit. Hell, he didn't care if she tore all of his hair out as long as she held on to him as if she'd drown without him.

"You are so sexy. So responsive." He kept her hovering on the edge, sawing his fingers in and out of her sheath as she looked at him in a daze, her lips parted in wonder.

On wobbly knees, he knelt between her thighs and ran his wet hand over his erection to smear her cream all over the stiff flesh, then positioned the head at her entrance.

She shifted her hips away with a gasp. "Trey, condom."

Her words barely penetrated the fog of sex surrounding him. A condom?

"No. No." He shook his head and placed the tip of his shaft inside her. "Nothing between us. Ever. Just you and me."

For a second, he thought he saw sadness flash in her eyes, but the ability to form any more thoughts ceased to exist as he pushed into her willing body. Damn, she was fist tight. And hot and so damn wet. He'd never felt anything better in his life. At only two inches in, his balls drew up tight, preparing to unload.

"God, Greta, you feel so good." Sweat broke out across his face and chest as he worked his way in deeper. He was afraid he wasn't going to last as he slid the last inch home.

It took all of his concentration not to move and give them both time to adjust, but Greta wasn't having any of that.

"Trey, please. Please move," she begged.

He couldn't, he was too close. He didn't want it to be over before it begun. Her fingernails scored down his back and over his ass. Fiery jolts trailed in their wake and made his hips jerk, pushing him deeper into her heat.

"Greta, don't," he warned. This was his show, and he wasn't letting her take over.

"Take me," she whispered before reaching between his legs to stroke his scrotum.

"Fuck." He bucked hard and picked up his pace. The more he plunged, the more of his body she touched and caressed, stoking the flames burning him alive. By the smile hovering on her lips, he knew she pushed him on purpose.

"You like this, you little witch. Don't you?" He punctuated his words with a sharp thrust of his hips. "Does your little pussy like it when I ride you hard?"

"Yes." Her smile widened then she shifted her hips to take him deeper, hissing with glee as he struck home. This was the hellcat he knew she could be. The woman who worked him up just so he could show her who was boss in the bedroom.

A ripple of warning shot from his cock up his spine. "Where

do you want me to come, baby?" Ripples rolled through her pussy and tugged at his length, readying for her own release.

"Inside me."

"Tell me where," he growled, getting closer. "I want to hear you say the word."

"In my pussy," she panted.

"Then you have to help pull the cum from me." He threw his head back and pounded away. Her head tossed back and her spine arched off the mattress. She hung on to his surging hips as she came, her eyes wide in shock. Her pupils were so large, all hints of the brown of her irises had disappeared.

Her clenching pussy sucked on his cock in hard pulls and gave him that final shove off the edge. He fell so hard, so fast, the bottom of his world dropped out. His only anchor was where they were joined as one. Plunging as deep as he could go, he filled her full of his seed, reclaiming his place as her lover.

Long minutes passed while they stared at each other in wonder. Tremors racked both of them as he floated back down to earth. The adrenaline crash made him remember his injured shoulder that was screaming in pain, but he refused to withdraw from her loving embrace. Wrapping her in his arms, he rolled them over so that she could rest against his uninjured side.

Good lord. His lungs billowed as he waited for his vision to clear. Greta was everything he wanted in and out of bed. She was so responsive, so passionate. Yet even at her most vulnerable, he still felt her holding back.

His woman was in his arms, his body was sated, but his mind wouldn't rest. Her earlier flash of sadness was a damper on his euphoria and reminded him there was a lot of history between them he couldn't remember. Perhaps in his other life he'd rather cut off his right arm than disturb the peace of the moment, but right now, he needed answers.

"Greta," he rasped out from his dry throat. "How long has it been since we've been together like that?"

The way she froze in his arms told him that he wasn't going to like the answer.

Chapter 10

T HE SEXUAL HIGH Greta had been riding plummeted in the wake of Trey's seemingly innocuous question. Tension invaded her bones, making her want to curl into a protective ball, but she fought the urge and forced her body to remain lax.

"What do you mean?" she asked, striving for casual confusion.

"How long has it been since we've made love?"

One year, three months, and seventeen days.

She remembered the night with devastating clarity. Luke's death had obliterated the foundation of their world. When she needed the strength of her husband's love to reassure her that they as a couple were all right, Trey had withdrawn, cutting her off from the one thing she had believed was infallible: his support.

Then one night Trey had come to her, taking her body with an urgency that matched her desperation to rebuild the connection they once shared. The fire of his kisses, the fervor in his touch banished the shadows of having her family torn asunder. Her husband had returned to her arms, and all was going to be just as it was.

Until the condom broke.

All of his warmth dissipated, once more leaving a cold shell that appeared to be more machine than man. He treated her as if she were made of spun sugar and likely to shatter with the slightest bump. Exactly twenty-eight days later he made her take a pregnancy test, then another, then another. After a week of negative results, he sighed an "amen" and never touched her again.

And now the man she married was back. She'd rather dive face first into a hot griddle before reminding him of that nightmare. It was painful enough to live through it the first time.

But Trey asked a question, and if he was truly getting back to his former self, he wasn't going to let her go without answering.

"A while, I guess." She shrugged. "You know, it's been crazy lately."

"Don't lie to me, and don't be coy. You were practically virgin tight, so I know it's been longer than a while. How long?"

She ran her fingers through the soft hair that ran from his navel to his groin. "Why does it matter?"

He grabbed her wrist in a firm grip. "Because it does. How long, Greta?"

The sound of the clock ticking on the nightstand grew louder and louder with each heartbeat. Neither of them moved.

"March," she lied. Hopefully, the fake date would appease his curiosity.

It didn't.

"Fuck! Sorry," he apologized when she flinched. "That was a fuck at me, not you." He sat up to look down at her, confusion pulling at his brow. "Why so long?"

"I don't know," she said, trying to keep the frustration and hurt out of her voice. She felt as though she might crack with him hovering over her. She sat up as well and hunched her shoulders, drawing her knees in tight.

"What do you suspect?" he asked.

She sucked in a watery breath. Days of stress had her emotions rolling just under the skin, and controlling them was becoming as difficult as riding a bicycle across a tightrope. "I truly don't know. One day you stopped touching me. At first I thought—" God, the things she imagined as she had tried to figure out what she had done to drive him away. "I thought you were having an affair, but then you rarely left the ranch, so I wasn't sure. You pretty much cut yourself off from everyone. Mark, the other hands. No one knew why."

"I'm sorry, Greta. It wasn't you. It had nothing to do with you." He placed a comforting hand on her shoulder.

"Don't say that." She rounded on him in a spark of anger and flung his hand off her skin. The leash on her control strained to the breaking point. "You don't know. You don't remember what happened, so don't patronize me."

"I'm not. I just know that if I pushed you away, it wasn't over anything you did."

"You just *know*." She smirked in disbelief. "Well, doesn't that just explain everything, then? Are you trying to stay on my good side in hopes of another easy lay?" she sneered.

"Don't," he barked. "Don't go there."

What was she doing? Why couldn't she keep her mouth shut? She should be seducing him, reminding him of the best of who they were, not dredging up the sordid details of their past. She thought she had worked through the pain of Trey's withdrawal. Apparently, she was dead wrong on that front. All of the hurt and embarrassment she had endured was rolling through her like an unchecked pot of water. Boiling and spitting until she felt as if she were a hair's breadth away from lashing out and destroying this tenuous connection. She had to get away from the pleading in his blue eyes before she ruined everything.

He caught her mid-leap as she tried to jump off the bed and panic set in. She pushed and thrashed in his hold, but who was she kidding? This was a man who wrestles cows for a living. She was no match for his strength, but still she struggled, fueled with the adrenaline of pure desperation.

"Greta, stop." He grabbed her hair in one hand and wrapped his other around her jaw to force her to look at him. "Don't make me hogtie you, because I will," he warned. "You're hurt and angry and I don't blame you. But don't go saying or assuming things you might regret. Can I remember the whys about anything I've done the past few years? No, but I have eyes and I can see. I've seen that hole of an office. I see how you don't trust me. It doesn't take a genius to figure out that I've been hiding. And I'm guessing that it started after Luke died."

She gasped in surprise at his intuition. He released her jaw to stroke the back of his fingers over her cheek. "I really am sorry. Something that should have brought us closer together, I let drive us apart."

One teardrop slipped from her eye and landed on his hand. When she turned away, he cuddled her closer and nuzzled her ear. "I have a feeling I'm gonna be apologizing for the rest of my life. But I'll do it. You deserve the best from me."

"How can you say that?" she whispered, her voice broken. "You don't know who I am."

"And I keep telling you that I do. I know that you're smart, you're talented. You love to laugh. I can see that when you love someone, you love them fiercely. Whatever memories are missing in my life, you fill that hole with the beauty that is you, Greta."

At his words, a sob broke free. The hand in her hair kept her from pulling away, though she tried her best to look everywhere but at him. For so long, she had waited for him to say those words, but how could she trust them? Trey was reacting on instinct. He didn't know their history. Would he feel the same way when he remembered?

"Look, magpie, whatever wrong happened between us, forget it. We're starting over. I want out of the darkness. I want a life with you." He pressed his forehead to hers. "No more hiding. Not for me and not for you."

She nuzzled his jaw with her cheek. "I'm afraid," she murmured against his skin.

"Me too, baby doll. But one day at a time, right?"

Her lips twitched as her words came back to her. "One day at a time."

Could it be so easy? She was so afraid to trust, to hope. But in her heart she knew she needed to take that last step of faith. They were partners. It would only work if both of them were committed.

Resolve settled over her and she straightened. She leaned against him and pressed her lips to his. Her promise.

His fingertips skimmed along her jaw and down across her collarbone, sending chills along her flesh. She stroked his hair before smoothing her palms over his shoulders and down his rock-hard abs. Long minutes passed as they traded soft caresses and gentle kisses until the need to be joined with him again, be one with him, became too much to bear.

Trey leaned back against the headboard and encouraged her to straddle his lap. The hard jut of his cock curved up to his belly, deliciously swollen and ready to be ridden. Her mouth watered, eager to lap at the juice leaking from the plum-shaped head, but her pussy was hungrier, ravenous for another taste of his salty seed.

She loved the way his eyelids grew heavy with desire and

those baby blues flamed when she took a firm grasp of his shaft, stroking her thumb under the glands as she settled her pussy over his cock and began the slow descent. The slide in was much easier than the time before. They were both panting heavily by the time he filled her to bursting.

She was so wet, her thighs slick with cream and wetting them both. It was always like that with Trey. He was the only man to make her melt with just a simple touch and a husky moan. He lit a fire within her that he alone controlled. And when he turned it up full bore, the flames consumed her from the inside out until he doused the inferno with hot blasts of his release. She belonged to him, body and soul, and she had been afraid she'd never feel the burn again.

"Damn, baby, you feel so good. I don't think it can get much better."

"Is that a challenge?" She picked up the pace.

"No." He stilled her hips with his hands. "Slow. Go slow. I want this to last all night."

Her smile felt more like a grimace as she struggled with her rising desire. "I don't think I can survive more."

"I bet you can. Come on, see if you can outlast me," he dared.

Challenge accepted. She swirled her hips and squeezed her inner muscles tight around his shaft.

His eyes rolled to the back of his head as he cursed. In retaliation, he cupped her breasts and tugged on her nipples.

She gritted her teeth. "Damn it, Trey."

His laugh was filled with sin until she clamped down on him and turned it into a groan. She kept up the tortuous pace, slowly taking him deep until he bottomed out, then squeezing tight as she slid back up.

Sweat ran down their bodies and their muscles trembled with

fatigue as they both fought being the first to break. A whimper broke free from her as her sheath rippled around his driving length and a storm gathered low in her belly. Triumph lit his features as he sensed her impending orgasm.

"That's it, baby. Squeeze me tight," he encouraged.

Not yet, not until this moment was branded in his memory.

She brushed his lips with her fingertip and pressed into his mouth. He sucked at her finger, swirling his tongue around and nipping at the soft pad. When she pulled it free, the digit glistened in the dim light. Reaching behind her and between his legs, she found his hidden hole and pushed inside.

"Fuck!" he shouted. His head jerked back and slammed against the wall. His eyes crossed and his cock jerked and swelled in her tightening sheath with an orgasm that went on and on.

Somehow he found the strength to move his hand. He found her clit and pinched hard. Her sultry laughter turned into a scream as she went over the edge in a freefall that stole her ability to think. A million fireballs raced through her veins, exploding out the top of her head and the points of her nipples as her greedy pussy sucked up every drop of his cum. He kept up the pressure, milking every second of her orgasm until they slumped together in a sweaty, heaving heap.

"You're evil," he muttered into her hair.

She managed a weak laugh. "I'm going to be so sore tomorrow."

"But in a good way, right?"

"Oh yeah," she sighed dreamily.

"You do know I'll be wanting to do that again. And often."

Will he? Will he, really?

She pushed the lingering doubt away. He wanted a new start and she loved him. Somehow she'd find the strength to give it to him.

He cradled her head close to his heart and placed a kiss to her forehead as he scooted down the bed with her draped over him like a blanket. "Sweet dreams, magpie."

"Good night, Trey."

In seconds, his chest rose and fell in a deep pattern of sleep, but rest eluded her. Too much was still unsettled, and moments like this might never come again. With the beat of his heart under her ear and the weight of his arms around her shoulders, she lay in her husband's arms and savored the occasion until the sky turned purple with the arrival of the new day.

Chapter 11

Seven years earlier...

H E WAS EITHER a genius or the biggest dumb-fuck to ever walk the face of the earth.
　　Ting.
This was going to work.
Ting.
It had to work.
Ting.
Trey bent and snagged a few more pebbles from the rock garden. It was eleven at night and he stood outside the house that Greta shared with her cousin and Mark's sister as if he were a lovesick teenager with his first crush. Or a skeevy, peeping Tom pervert who hoped to catch a glimpse of skin through the curtains, depending on how you looked at it. Either way, this was a new experience for him.

A week had passed since that night of the Harvest Festival. During all that time, he couldn't get the woman, or that kiss, out of his head. She haunted his every thought, waking and dreaming. He imagined countless ways he'd show her exactly how good it could be between them, and he was desperate to try every one. She was his match and he'd be a fool to let her walk away without convincing her to give him a chance, which was why he came up with this brilliant idea of tossing rocks at her window.

Ting.

Sure, he could have rung the doorbell, but then he'd have had to face the cock-block twins. Melody and Gina had been trying to get into his jeans for years. Well, Melody not so much because of Mark, but Gina was not so subtle about her interest. Convincing Greta to go out with him was going to be difficult enough without the girl's constant flirting.

"Come on, come on, come on." He kissed the last pebble for luck then tossed it into the air.

The window opened just before the pebble hit the glass. Greta ducked as it sailed past her head. "What the hell?" She peered out into the night. "Trey? What are you doing?"

"I wanted to see you."

"Is there something wrong with the front door?"

"No. I just didn't want to disturb Gina or Melody."

She looked over her shoulder into the shadowy room, then back to him. He could barely make out her features in the moonlight, but he thought he saw an amused smirk curl her lip. "And a phone wouldn't work because..."

"I don't know your number. And would you have talked to me on the phone?"

She lowered her gaze and bit her lip. After a second, she shrugged. "Maybe."

"Ha, see, that's why the window. Come on. It's a nice night. Come take a walk with me."

"Why?"

"I want to talk to you. Get to know you." *Strip you naked and kiss every inch of that delectable body, but I can't do that until you get within kissing distance.*

"Trey," she said with a sigh that seemed to come from her toes. "You know I don't do short term."

"It's just a walk. I want to be your friend. We can be friends, right? What are you afraid of?" He smiled in that cocky way he knew would rile her. "Do you think that if you spend more than three minutes with me, you'll fall so in love that you'll never want to leave?"

Her lips tightened. "No." She folded her arms, pushing her full breasts together, drawing his gaze. "Just a walk?"

"Just a walk." For now. "Come on. Rapunzel, Rapunzel, let down your hair." She didn't move a muscle. "Romeo, Romeo, wherefore art thou, Romeo?"

Finally, a genuine smile and a ring of laughter. "That's a little backwards, but I'll give you credit for the effort." She held up a finger. "Don't move."

The window closed with a snap, and then the light went out. As he stood in the bushes, the thrum of excitement quickened his blood. The air felt crisper and the stars in the night sky appeared sharper. Honeysuckle and apples filled the air with a sweet scent that tickled his nostrils as he scuffed his boots in the gravel and waited. And waited. What was taking her so long? He was about to go around to the front of the house when she appeared from around the corner.

She wore a denim skirt, cowboy boots, and a gray hoodie over a blue cotton T-shirt. On any other woman the outfit might have looked frumpy, but with her smooth bare legs, her impeccable posture, and that swing of her hips, she looked as sexy as sin. Damn, the woman knew how to walk. At the festival, Greta had looked like Rodeo Drive in her red dress, all style and sophistication, and that hadn't changed with the more casual outfit. But now she looked ready to take a tumble in the back of his truck, and that was more than all right with him.

"So." She stopped, keeping a foot of distance between them. Closer than he expected her to stand after her hands-off attitude. "You want to be my friend."

"That's right," he drew out slowly. The little witch was up to something.

"Interesting." She looped her arm around his elbow and pulled him along. He felt her heat all along his side where they touched. The softness of her breast brushed against his arm, with each step making his cock grow hard. It was going to be an uncomfortable walk. "So, what do you want to talk about, *girlfriend*? How about why aren't you out whooping it up on a Friday night?"

"Whooping?" he chuckled. "You know the word 'whooping'?"

"I've heard it bandied about around here." When she smiled, her whole face lit up, and her eyes sparkled with secrets that made you feel as if she was sharing them only with you. "But seriously, no date?"

Like anyone could hold his attention after her. "I don't date as much as you think. Running a ranch is an exhausting business, especially when it's your ranch. It's been worth it, though. Things are starting to go really well. Today I met with some people who are interested in my semen."

Greta tripped. "What?"

"My—" he broke off when he realized what he said, and the tips of his ears began to burn. "Bull semen. They want to breed from my bulls."

Her laugh echoed into the night, dark and rich. She gripped his arm tight with one hand while the other braced against her knee. He laughed with her, captivated by the way her amusement engulfed her entire body.

He brushed the tears from his eyes with the sleeve of his

jacket. "Sorry. Forgot that you might not know what that means."

"Well, I do now." She straightened and pressed her hand against her side. "Oh my God, I haven't laughed that hard in a while." They resumed their stroll while she caught her breath. "Congratulations. It must be good to know that someone wants your semen."

"I have plenty of it and am eager to share," he teased, hoping she'd take the bait.

The only acknowledgment of his humor was a smile as she bumped his hip with hers. "Do you like ranching, or was it something you felt like you had to take on?"

"I love it. I do." He was encouraged that she was asking questions about his life, showing an interest in him. "It's all I've ever known, but it's also all I've wanted to do. I love the open air, the sun beating on my back. I love the way I feel worn out and tired at the end of a good day's work. Where else can I call Mother Nature my office?" He grinned at her and when she smiled back, a match struck inside him, warming his heart. She listened to him, completely open and engaged. "I always knew that someday the 'A' would be mine. I just wished it hadn't been so soon."

"I heard about your parents. I'm sorry. I can't imagine the pressure and responsibility you must have felt taking on the ranch like that at so young an age." She squeezed his biceps. He placed his free hand over hers and was delighted when she didn't pull away.

"It was rough, really rough for a while. Mark was a big help. I couldn't have done it without him." He frowned when he saw that they had already gone around the block and come back to her front door.

"That's good that you have such a great friendship. I was

never close to anyone that way. I spent most of my time in a library or art studio. It tends to lead to an isolated existence. Well," She glanced at the door, then at him before pulling away. "That was nice. Thank you."

She was dead wrong if she thought he would let her leave with only a "That's nice" comment. "Wait up, woman. We're not done yet. I haven't had a chance to get to know about you."

Her dark eyes stared up at him, assessing, scrutinizing. Trey held still. This was another one of her tests. He didn't know what she was looking for when she gazed at him that way, but he didn't want to give her any reason to turn him away. "Okay." She must have seen something she liked. "Would you like to come in for some cocoa?"

"Cocoa?" The question surprised him. He would have expected a glass of wine or some fancy coffee.

"Yes, cocoa. You know, chocolate, milk." She really did seem to love giving him a hard time.

"I know what it is. We won't be disturbing the girls, will we?"

"It's Friday. They're out on dates."

"Really?" He tried to keep the joy in his tone to a minimum. More alone time with Greta? Now that was a happy change of plans. "I would love to try your cocoa."

She said nothing, just smiled that secret smile of hers and let him in.

The little two-story rental was worn but cozy. The scent of apple pie and cinnamon welcomed him when he entered and reminded him of his mother's cooking. He followed Greta into the kitchen and watched as she took out a small pot and a cutting board. She looked very comfortable in her environment while she gathered her ingredients.

"Why no date for you on a Friday?" he asked leaning against

the counter. She glanced over her shoulder with an imperiously raised eyebrow. "Ah, yes. That's right. You don't do short term."

"See, you can learn. Cookie?" She placed a plate of oatmeal raisin cookies next to him and then went back to the stove to heat the milk.

"I don't see how you're going to find Mr. Long Term if you don't even give Mr. Short Term a try." He bit into a cookie. "Hot damn. These are delicious. What brand are they?"

She laughed. "I made them."

"Are you kidding?" They were the tastiest thing he ever ate. Moist, chewy, not too sweet with just the right amount of salt to make him want another, and another. "These are really good." He watched with amusement as she grated the block of chocolate before stirring it into the simmering milk. No powdered mixes for Greta—it was obvious she took her food seriously.

"Thank you. I like to cook. It's another way to express my creativity. Just a second. This is going to be loud." She took a bowl down from the cupboard and a carton of cream from the refrigerator. She whipped the cream with a hand mixer until a white mountain formed in the bowl. A dollop of whipped cream went into each of their steaming mugs. "Here you go. Shall we go sit on the couch?"

"Absolutely." He followed the sway of her denim encased hips into the living room. He couldn't help it. Watching her in action in the kitchen, looking very domestic, turned him on. It called to the caveman inside him that made him want to pound his chest and shout "Good mate, go claim."

He let her pick her seat before he sat down beside her on the couch, leaving enough space between them so that she wouldn't feel crowded, but close enough he could make out her nipples poking through her thin T-shirt. She had taken the hoodie off when they returned, and the cotton-covered mounds beckoned to him to come and rest his weary head. *Soon, my beauties*, he promised.

"You didn't answer my question about why no date for you," he reminded her. He took a sip, and the rich chocolate slid across his tongue, smooth and creamy. "Wow, that's good. Stop distracting me with food."

She giggled and grinned at him from behind her mug. "I'm not doing anything."

"Then answer the question."

"I told you. I am only here for a few months. That's not enough time to properly cultivate a relationship."

"But what if the man for you is right here? You're just going to let him go because you don't think there's enough time for whatever it is you want to cultivate?"

"And you think that man is you?"

"Yes."

She laughed again and rested her head against the cushion, her gaze on the ceiling. When she caught her breath she looked back at him with admiration and exasperation in her gaze. "You don't hold back, do you?"

"Nope. Life's too short. You have to grab it before it passes you by. So why are you going to let me go?"

"Look, Trey." She placed her mug on the table, and then pushed the hair off her face before turning to him. "I've seen it happen. To my mother, to all of my married friends. They marry men who have really big, life-encompassing careers. Then their wants become his wants, and their friends are only his friends. They give up everything that made them special and unique for the sake of making their man happy. Their essence was sucked from them, leaving them with nothing."

"You think I'm going to suck out your essence?" He was

having a hard time following her train of thought. She spoke with passion, so he knew it was important enough that he had to concentrate on what she was saying.

Whatever expression she saw on his face made her laugh again. "Maybe not intentionally, but before long it would turn into me staying at the ranch, cleaning, cooking for your men. No chance to make any of my jewelry. You wouldn't want me going out because you'd want me home to tell me about your day and watch the kids and take care of the house. Then everything that made me *me*—poof. Gone. I don't want that."

"Is that why you turned Mark down, too?"

She sighed and lowered her gaze. "Partly. He seems nice. And he is good looking. He really knows how to rock that whole tall, dark, and handsome thing." A tick began near his eye as wickedness touched the curve of her smile. "And those cheekbones are to die for. He looks so intense. I guess that could be a good thing, though. Do you think he's an intense lover?"

"I wouldn't know," he gritted out between clenched teeth.

"Hmm." She looked contemplative for a moment before returning to her answer. "Mark has that vibe. You know, 'Don't worry, little lady, I'll take care of everything.' It's very over-whelming. And I don't want to be 'taken care of.' I want to be involved too. Plus, there was no spark."

"Spark?"

"Yeah, you know what I mean, *girlfriend*." She smiled and clasped her hands to her breast. "That spark from when your hands touch and the electricity shoots up your arm and your insides turn all mushy."

He rested his arm along the back of the couch in a decep-tively casual pose. The woman could teach a course in how to drive him crazy. "Oh yeah, like when I see a beautiful woman in a red dress and my stomach starts to roll and my cock gets hard enough to hammer nails. I know exactly what you mean. *Girlfriend.*" He winked and let loose with a big, toothy grin.

She turned away, biting her lip. "You are too much." She wanted to laugh, he could see it, but she just shook her head. "Too much."

"Greta." He set his mug down and leaned toward her. "I get what you're saying. I really do. That won't happen with me. I like that we're different. Makes it interesting. You can make all the jewelry you want, whole truckloads if that makes you happy. I just want to be with you. What's wrong with that?"

Confusion and uncertainty swirled in her eyes when she met his gaze. "Nothing, Trey. Nothing. I think it's nice you believe you can be that kind of man."

Goddammit, the woman was going to make him punch a hole in the wall. "Trust. It's an issue of trust. Is it just me or all men?"

"Of course I don't trust you. I don't know you."

He bit back his curse, his hands trembled with the need to strangle her. "If you get to know me, then you'll trust me." He reached across the couch and took her hand. A jolt raced up his arm as he heard her gasp. They both stared at their clasped hands, their breaths loud and harsh in the quiet room. "Look. Sparks."

Greta jumped to her feet. Trey let her get two steps away before he banded an arm around her waist and pulled her tight into the curve of his body. Her rapid breathing would have had him thinking she was hyperventilating, except he felt the same way. Lightning struck whenever they touched. It was intense, like bungee jumping off a bridge, fascinating and frightening at the same time.

"Don't run. Don't be afraid." He pressed his lips to her ear.

She trembled in his arms, both of her hands holding tight to his forearms. "Greta, you're like a comet. Spectacular and rare. The kind that takes seventy-five years to come back around. Do you think I'm not gonna try to catch your tail, just to experience your fire? Enjoy the beauty that is you? I'd be a fool. Take the leap with me. I won't let you fall."

Another shudder shook her. "I want to. You make me want to." She turned her head. Her nose brushed along his jaw. "I don't know what to do." The tremor in her voice told him how out of her comfort zone she was, but she wasn't fighting him.

"I'll never make you regret trusting me, Greta. I promise."

He put his heart in his eyes and let her see his sincerity. The blood pounded in his head so fiercely he was afraid he'd drop with a stroke from the pressure. If this night taught him anything, it was that Greta did not do anything by half measures. When she gave herself to him, it would be with her whole heart. Patience with her would be well worth the effort.

When she lifted her face for his kiss, he knew she was his. He had won, they had won, and now it was time for her to collect her prize. It killed him to go slow, but he did. He wanted to savor every moment. She said she was leaving in a few weeks. He was determined to give her a reason to stay.

He took care to find the perfect fit for their mouths. Chocolate and that spice he already associated as belonging to Greta filled his senses. He didn't devour her, he didn't consume her. He sipped, he savored.

The entire evening had been an exercise in studying Greta. She was a tactile person, sensuous in her movement. The way she held onto his arm during their walk, how she trailed her finger over the counter as she cooked and the rim of her mug as she drank. She touched, she felt, because she liked to be touched in return. That observation was confirmed when he traced his thumb along her jaw and cupped her neck in his palm. She sighed into his mouth and let him take all of her weight as she sagged against him. The hand he trailed down her back and around her hip had her arching and mewling like a kitten being stroked.

Together they fell onto the couch, Trey sitting and Greta straddling his left thigh. The heat of her skin enticed him to touch and explore. Over her shirt he palmed her breast. The heavy weight filled his hand as if it were made for him. When he pulled and plucked her nipple through the lace and cotton, she reared up with a hiss. Her eyes glittered in the lamplight while her lips, wet and swollen, curled into a satisfied grin. "Your kisses have gotten better."

"I told you, I'm a quick study." He pinched the nub harder in retaliation of her doubt. She responded by grinding her hot pussy against his leg. The evidence of her arousal singed his nerves. "Jesus, I knew you were a wildcat."

Her husky chuckle shot straight to his groin. The warmth of her breath touched his neck just before her teeth scraped over his pulse. His hips jerked in reaction, making her laugh again. With slow deliberation, she ran her hand down his chest to rest low on his belly. Her fingernail tapped the top snap on his jeans. The tiny vibration zinged along the shaft. "How are you at sex? Are you better than your kisses would suggest?"

"Baby doll, don't you know not to tease a bull?"

"Is that the same as don't grab one by the horns?" Her hand squeezed his length through his jeans.

"She-devil," he groaned, then pulled her shirt up and over her head and flipped her down to the couch so fast she actually squeaked.

She blinked up at him from her new position flat on her back. "Impatient?" she gasped.

"You have no idea." He rained kisses from her collarbone to the swells of her breast. "I've been dreaming about this all week."

The white lace of her bra glowed against his tanned hands as he pulled the cups down to expose her dusky nipples. She was a feast waiting to be tasted. He bent to sample her treats, reveling in the way she bucked and rolled beneath him. Under his callused palms she was living satin. A sparkling gem in his grubby workman's hands. He'd never be worthy to touch such perfection, but there was no way in hell he would ever give her up.

"I want to touch you, too," she panted. She managed to unzip his jeans, her hand coming to rest just above his groin. Her fingers tugged the hairs around the base, a sensation that had his eyes rolling into the back of his head.

"Please, please, please, please." It took him a while to figure out the begging was coming from him.

She rewarded him by wrapping those talented fingers around his girth. Firm, long strokes brought him to the brink too quickly. He gritted his teeth and fought the urge to spill. The little witch's throaty laugh told him that she was enjoying driving him mad. Well, two could play at that game.

His fingers found her silk panties wet with need. He pushed the fabric aside and traced the lips of her sex. She giggled and moaned at the same time while adding a twist to her wrist with every down stroke. Between the laughter and moans they traded teasing caresses, each driving the other higher, daring the other to break first. He pressed two thick fingers deep inside her wet heat. God, she was tight. If he weren't careful, he would blow before his cock was all the way in. She was so responsive, giving as good as she got.

"What do you want?" he breathed against her lips. "Tell me

what you want, Greta."

"You, Trey." She lifted up to nip at his mouth. "I want you to fuck me."

Her words inflamed and chilled him at the same time. She was right where he wanted her, yet so far away. He settled between her thighs and rubbed his aching cock against her pussy, pushing the silk of her panties into her slit. He wrapped her thick hair around his hand so he could hold her still. Dark eyes drowsy with desire gazed up at him.

"I'm not going to fuck you, Greta." He thrust his hips, showing her how much he wanted her. "I'm going to make love to you. Never think that it's anything different between us."

Her kiss-swollen lips parted with surprise and her eyes widened. She swallowed hard. "I know, Trey. I wouldn't expect anything less from you." Gently, she brushed a lock of hair from his forehead, then trailed her fingers down his cheek.

Pure joy burst from his chest. She *did* understand. His mouth claimed her, staked his territory while he reached for his wallet in his back pocket. He couldn't believe how much his hands shook at the prospect of having her.

"Greta, are you still up?"

"Motherfucker," Trey growled. Every muscle in his body screamed at the abrupt change of blood flow. His arms gave out as he collapsed, smothering Greta with his weight.

Gina strolled into the living room as she shed her jacket. "Well, that was a wasted evening. Cheap dinner and a tiny dick—Trey? My, my, my. Trey Armstrong, what are you doing here?"

"He was about to entertain me with his not-tiny dick." Greta leveled a gimlet glare at her cousin over the back of the couch. "Do you mind? We would like some privacy."

"Oh, come on. It looks like the party's just getting started.

What say we give Trey a really good time?" Gina purred.

Seriously? Did Greta even swing that way?

Normally, the idea of two beautiful women willing to pleasure him would have had him raring to go, but now it had his stomach clenching with distaste. Damn, he must really like this girl.

Greta dug her fingers into the hair at the nape of his neck and cradled him to her breast. Whether it was to let him know she was all right or to use him as a cover up, he didn't know. Nestled against her like that, he really didn't care. He just wanted to recapture that perfect moment when she gave herself to him.

"I say you leave. Now." Greta's tone brokered no argument.

"Oh, you so don't know how to have fun." Gina stormed off in a huff. The sharp click of her heels echoed down the hall like machine-gun fire.

He couldn't stop the moan of loss that rippled from his throat. Her chest bounced with her suppressed laughter. "You do know that she's probably listening outside the door?" she whispered right into his ear.

"I wouldn't doubt that." He kept his tone just as low to prevent Gina from getting her jollies.

"Do you think you could keep quiet?" She flexed her thighs around his hips.

He snorted. "With you? Never. I have no restraint when it comes to you, magpie."

"Magpie?" Her fingers kept stroking his hair like she couldn't get enough of touching him.

"Yeah. Margaret, you like to cook and bake pies, and you like to talk things out. Magpie."

"I've never let anyone give me a cutesy nickname."

"You like it when I do it. I can tell by the goose bumps on your arms and the way your nipples pucker when I call you 'baby doll.' " Said nipples beaded to attention, begging to be licked. He shook his head to clear it. "You better cover up, or I'll forget my place and take you right now, never mind the audience."

"Your strength amazes me." She giggled and sat up, smoothing her clothes back into place. He almost whimpered when she covered her magnificent breasts but knew it wasn't the last he'd see of them. "We're getting dressed now. Good night, Gina," she called out.

A muffled "damn" came from the hallway, followed by the heavy tread of stocking feet.

Not wanting to let her go just yet, he pulled her close once they were dressed. She rested along his side as though she was meant to be there. "Tomorrow night, come to the ranch. I'll show you around. We can pack a picnic."

"Okay."

"There's this perfect spot right along the stream under this huge elm tree, and—what did you say?"

She laughed. "I said okay."

"Really? I don't have to convince you to spend time with me?"

"Oh, Trey," she sighed and brushed his hair back again. "It was never an issue of not wanting to spend time with you. I like you."

"Good." Was all he said, trying to remain cool, but not able to stop the warmth that infused him and had him grinning like a fool.

He couldn't resist the provocative pull of her lips. He kissed her with a mixture of elation and desire. She was with him. She made her choice, and she was running with it. His fingers dug into her side as the need arose in him again and the twitch in his erection reminded him of the aborted attempt to make love to her. Reluctantly, he drew away, his willpower stretched paper thin when he saw the sheen on her lips left by his kiss. "I better go. I'll see you tomorrow then?"

The light in her eyes and the promise in her smile made his breath catch. "Tomorrow."

TREY AWOKE WITH a start. The room was encased in darkness save for the numbers on the alarm clock glowing 4:00. Greta was curled against his side, soft and warm, just where she belonged. He grinned, his hand stroking her thick hair.

She'd been quite the little spitfire back then. Where had that woman who was so direct and held nothing back gone? The woman who looked at every angle then threw herself in wholeheartedly? It made him sad to think that he had done something to dampen her spirit.

But she was with him now. Persistence and willingness to learn. That was what she claimed had gained her trust all those years ago. Well, he'd always prided himself on being a good student. If it worked once, it would work again.

Right?

Chapter 12

"GRETA, WHAT IS this?"

She poked her head around Trey's tall body and looked down at the smoldering hot grill, where he poked at a pink rectangle with the tongs. "Steak, chicken, and salmon."

"Salmon?" Did the woman not know where she lived? "Baby doll, you can't have fish next to steak. It's against the laws of nature."

"Watch it there, Hoss." Mark handed him a beer. "Greta's salmon is my favorite thing she makes."

"Really? That good?" When you lived out in cattle country, fish was sometimes synonymous with a four-letter word.

Mark nodded. "That good."

Greta handed Trey a spatula. "Watch the grill. I'm going to get the fruit salad."

"Hey." He caught her by the elbow and pulled her in for a quick kiss. "Don't take too long."

She was able to contain the grin that tugged on her lips, but a blush blossomed across her cheeks. All day long she had resembled her old self, the one Trey remembered, carefree and dazzling, and even he felt more rejuvenated. His reflection in the mirror looked more like that young man from the picture in his office. Apparently, great sex did do a body good.

Both men watched her hips sway as she walked into the house as Trey ignored the snickers and catcalls from the rest of the hands standing behind him. The woman did wear denim well.

"You're looking quite spry," Mark commented. "Things going well, I take it?"

"Yeah." Trey laughed with unrestrained joy. "Yeah." There was a good chance that the huge grin on his face would become permanent.

Spending the day with Greta, laughing and kissing while preparing for the cookout, taught him several invaluable lessons. He noticed more about her in those few hours than his twenty-three year old self would have observed. Young Trey had been all about her beauty, how different she was from the other girls in Mission, and those gorgeous tits. Older, more mature Trey saw her inner strength, her compassion, the great love she had for those around her. He admired how she took the time and energy to think of others. Earlier that morning he watched as she finished the necklace she made for Adam's mother. Saw the detail and care she took to make sure it looked exactly how he wanted. She created a menu to have each of his men's favorite dish at the cookout. Greta made the effort to care.

And through all of that, she never let Trey out of her sight. She guided his hand while working on supper, whether he needed it or not, with that tiny grin on her face as if she just needed a reason touch him. He caught her gazing at him with wonder and hope in her eyes that left his insides shaking. She was opening up like a rare flower, retaking her place by his side. It had been a great day.

"Have you remembered anything new?" Mark took a draw

off his beer, watching him closely.

"I've remembered enough." He turned around to observe the group that had gathered near the fire. He spread out his arms to encompass the group. "This. This I remember. Well, maybe not these men specifically, but you know what I mean."

All of his men were there, along with Adam's and Steven's girlfriends. Jokes were swapped, stories told, just like the cookouts his parents had put on when he was a kid.

"I can't feel like I'm missing out or suffering by not remembering everything. I'm alive. I have a great woman. Business is good, and I have my best friend at my side. Life doesn't get better than this, Hoss."

"That's you, Trey. The golden boy." Mark smiled, although it appeared to Trey as if it was forced.

He glanced around again. "No date tonight for you, Hoss?"

A blank curtain fell across his face. "Nope."

"Why not?"

The muscles in Mark's jaw bunched with tension. "None of the women around here interest me."

"Well, what kind of woman are you looking for?" Trey knew he sounded harpy, but he couldn't help it. He was just so damn happy, and he wanted Mark to have some of that happiness, too.

A wave of annoyance rolled off Mark as he shifted his stance. "I want a woman who is kind, intelligent, loyal, and hard working. I'd want her to love me so much that she'd walk through hell for me, because I certainly would for her." The timber of his voice was low and intense.

"Wow." Trey could only blink at the fire in Mark's stare. "She sounds like she'd be quite a woman."

Mark's mouth tightened as he nodded.

"Hey, boys! Watch the steaks!" Greta shouted as she placed a huge bowl on the picnic table.

Trey and Mark jumped and flipped the smoldering steaks in the nick of time. The scent of grilled meat and roasted spices hovered like an epicurean cloud waiting to rain its scrumptious flavors down upon them. Trey's stomach growled. Mark's stomach growled. Behind them the shifting of the crowd grew, building with tension. The natives were ravenous.

"Dinner's ready everyone," Greta announced.

Like a pack of locusts, they descended on the food. Steve and Colby didn't even bother with plates and utensils and started stuffing salads and biscuits straight into their mouths.

Greta stopped Trey by waving a full fork of pink meat in front of his nose. "Here, try this."

"What is it?" he asked dubiously. "Is that your fish?"

"Just try it," she cajoled. When he opened his mouth with hesitation, she placed the bite of grilled teriyaki salmon on his tongue.

Well, whatd'ya know. The hot salmon melted in his mouth, crispy-sweet and salty and absolutely delicious. He wrapped his arms around her and leaned down to rub noses. "I am sorry I ever doubted your salmon."

Her eyes sparkled with laughter even as she pressed her lips together to stop from grinning. "You're forgiven." She kissed the corner of his mouth. "If you want some more, you better hurry. It's almost gone."

"Ah, hell no." He rushed to the table just in time to snatch the last piece.

Conversation reduced to contented moans and appreciative sighs. The sky performed a spectacular show as the sun set in a fiery splendor before settling into periwinkle twilight. A bonfire crackled and popped, warming them as they sat around on fallen logs and lawn chairs. Summer days in Central Washington reached into the nineties, but when the sun fell, the temperature became downright chilly. Trey was grateful to have Greta there to cuddle with and keep him warm.

Around mouthfuls of chicken and strawberry salad, Trey became reacquainted with his men. It still amazed him there were so many faces he didn't remember.

Colby had come to the ranch three years before. He grew up in Yakima and was the son of a veterinarian. He went to school to study animal husbandry and found out he liked riding the animals more than treating them, so he thought he would try his hand at ranching. He appeared on the shy side, more content to watch than participate. An air of innocence clung to him, and his bashful nature reminded Trey more of a teenager than an adult.

Adam had come on at the beginning of the year. Adam was the all-American boy next door. Blond and good looking, he had grown up in Mission and played high school football. He laughed all the time at everything. Trey didn't think anything got him down, except when he talked about his brother who had gone missing in action. The only questionable thing about Adam was his choice in girlfriends. Tanya giggled a little too loud, simpered a little too much, and reminded Trey of all the things he hadn't wanted in a mate. Not that he'd anything disparaging against the girl, but he really hoped Adam was not thinking long term with that one.

From what Trey pieced together, Jack had joined the ranch about the same time as Adam.

Jack had been a rodeo man and had competed on the circuit until he was stepped on by a bull. It took years for him to recover from the shattered femur, and he never sat on bull again. His skill with the rope made up for his lack of speed. He had an easy grin and a laidback style about him that Trey sensed was a cover. There was a power, an intensity coiled under his devil-may-care attitude, that appeared ready to unleash at any moment.

Trey had been on the receiving end of enough of those probing stares the last few days that he wondered if they'd ever had a falling out in the past. Jack hadn't mentioned anything, so Trey did his best to ignore the sensation.

At the moment Jack and Steven stood off to the side, taking turns lassoing the metal calf Trey's father had built long ago for him to practice his roping skills. However, when he was a boy, his dad hadn't made him take shots of whiskey when he missed. At the rate Steven was going, a real cow would have a better chance of roping him.

The kid was a good hand, but he always seemed to be just a half step behind everyone else, which Jack took advantage of when he got the chance. Steven planned on going to college in the fall to study engineering. The boy wanted to build bridges. Trey stumbled upon two of his structures out in the field and he really hoped Steven's real bridges held up better than the straw versions he saw crumbling out near the feed shed.

These were good men, his men, he thought with pride, and smiled at the group laughing around the fire. The ranch was like a tiny nation, and he was pleased with the soldiers he had defending his land.

Trey went back to the picnic table for seconds and ran into Jack, who was helping himself to a quarter of a chocolate cake. "Hey."

"Hey." Jack nodded. "Remember anything new?"

That was the most popular question of the evening. "A few things here and there."

"Uh-huh," Jack drew out in a long doubtful drawl. He added a slice of pie to his plate while keeping that ice-blue gaze locked on Trey, chilling him to the bone.

Trey took a quick glance around to see if anyone was within earshot before leaning in with a frustrated growl. "What's the deal, Jack?"

"What do ya mean?" He had the gall to lick icing off his thumb, acting as if he hadn't a clue he was pushing Trey's buttons, yet the unholy gleam in his eyes suggested different.

"Have I wronged you somehow in the past?"

"Not really." He shrugged.

"Then what's with the attitude?"

He raised a brow. "Why do you care? It's not like we're friends. As long as you get the work out of me you want, you pretty much couldn't care less about what I do and say."

"That's not true. Of course I'd want you to be happy here, Jack."

"Yeah, right."

"I'm serious," Trey said. He didn't know who he was more pissed at, Jack with the chip on his shoulder, or himself for letting his man feel that his blood, sweat, and effort weren't valued. "Why stay if you don't like it here?"

Jack sighed and scratched at the stubble on his chin. "Look, you're a hard-hearted, slave-driving SOB, but I can respect that because you're the boss. It's your ranch, and you know what you're doing when it comes to ranching." His eyes flicked over to where Greta sat talking to Mark. "But you're a shitty husband. I've stayed because of Mark, and Ben, and the rest of the guys. And Greta. I don't believe this little Trey sunshine routine I've seen that last few days. She's a good woman who deserves better than you."

"Someone like you, you mean." Trey felt as if he'd taken a flying leap into an icy river. His blood froze and brain functions slowed as he tried to picture the man Jack described. He wanted to refute everything Jack said, but in his gut he feared that since he returned from the hospital, Jack was the only person who was telling him straight-up the truth.

"Hell no. She's too good for me, too."

"Jack, I'm sorry. I...I don't know—I don't know what to say. But I can see that this ranch wouldn't be the success it is without you. As for Greta, well, I know she deserves better, and I'm gonna do everything I can to make sure she gets it. That's a promise."

"I'm not the one you need to make that promise to."

"No, I'm making it to you, too. You deserve to work for a man you can trust will do the best for everyone, including his men."

The tension in Jack's shoulders eased as he stared long and hard at Trey. It reminded him of Greta and her secret tests. He held still and let the determination in his gaze convey his sincerity. After several seconds, Jack nodded and headed back to the fire pit.

With his appetite ruined, Trey threw his plate into the garbage and fought the urge to throw up the wonderful feast. Did everyone believe he was an asshole? God, he hoped not, but there was so much evidence to the contrary that he had a suspicion he had a lot to make up for, and Greta was just the beginning.

Hiding from the problem wouldn't help, in fact, hiding was probably what dug him in the shit hole he was in to start with. To get back into his family's good graces, he would have to let his actions speak louder than words, which meant hauling his ass back to the fire pit with a smile on his face and join in on the festivities.

"Trey, are you all right?" Greta looped her arm around his elbow.

"I'm fine. Stuffed, but fine." He snuggled closer to her warmth.

"Hey, Ben, whatcha got there?" Steven asked as Ben

emerged from the darkness.

"I thought we might like some mood music." He settled his large frame on a fallen log and began to tune the guitar he carried. At six-four and two hundred-fifty pounds of pure muscle, the instrument looked like a toy in his big hands. When the notes rang to his liking, he began to play with a dexterity Trey didn't think possible for such thick fingers.

"What's that song?" Steven frowned.

" 'Tumbleweeds.' "

"Never heard of it."

Half of the group choked on their beers. "It's a classic," Trey snorted. "Even I remember that one."

"Do you know any Brad Paisley or Toby Keith?"

"Sure." Ben deftly plucked out the rockin' notes of "High Maintenance Woman." Steven whooped and pulled his girlfriend to her feet. He began to flail and gyrate his limbs like he was holding on to the wrong end of a cattle prod.

Adam rescued his beer before it was sacrificed to the dancing gods. "Watch out! White man dancing."

"Well then stand up and show me your goods, or are you chicken?"

"Stand back, Opie, it is so on." Adam had his girlfriend up and shaking to the music. His pinched face and jerky arms looked like he was suffering from muscle spasms. A one-legged monkey jumping on a bed of hot coals had more grace and style than those two.

Greta laughed so hard, she bent over double with her arms hugging her belly.

"Do we need to show them how it's done, baby doll?" Trey held out a hand.

"Oh." She wiped the tears from her cheeks. "I don't know if I can stand."

"Come on." Before she could blink, he had them twirling and swinging in smooth movements. With the stars overhead, he was back in Martinez's Orchard with the prettiest girl at the party smiling up at him.

Whistles rent the air along with jovial hooting and hollering. After he laid her out in a low dip, Greta tossed back her hair and let loose with a laugh straight from her soul. Her eyes sparkled and her cheeks flushed bright pink. She looked exactly like she had the night they met. This was the woman he remembered.

"Come over here, Ms. Margaret." Ben patted the seat next to him. "Let's see how much of the Irish is still in you."

"Ah, it's been a while," Greta warned as she took her place.

Ben strummed an introduction then nodded for her to begin.

"Will you go lassie, go. And we'll all go together..." Her voice rang pure and clear across the backyard as she sang about love found and lost. The light of the fire flickered on her face, casting her in an angelic glow.

Trey sat back in surprise. "She sings too?" he asked Mark who sat beside him.

He pulled a long draw on the cigarette he just lit then let out the smoke in a long stream. "She sings."

Ben joined her in the chorus, his deep bass blending sweetly with her soprano.

Trey closed his eyes and let the music wash over him. As he listened, a vision danced behind his eyelids of Greta laid out on a blue-and-green plaid blanket under the elm tree by the stream. Sunlight spilled through the leaves, painting random patterns on her naked body. Her sun-warmed nipples were hot against his tongue as he made love to her out in the open air. Afterward, when they were sated and spent, she cradled him to her breast and sang to him while she ran her fingers through his hair.

He also saw her in the kitchen humming along with the

radio. And again, sitting in a rocking chair. A bundle rested in her arms as she sang a soft lullaby. The blanket rustled and a little hand reached out to grasp her finger.

His eyes flew open on a gasp and his heart pounded behind his ribs. That wasn't his imagination, but his own memories. He remembered Luke.

"Wow, Ms. Greta, I didn't know you could sing." Steven's voice broke through Trey's elation.

"You're pretty good," Adam agreed. "You should sing more often."

Adam's comment stuck Trey like a knife through the heart. The boys were wrong. Greta sang all of the time. If the radio was on, she sang. When she cooked, she sang. He remembered. He honestly remembered Greta singing. They would have had to have heard her at some point.

"Are you all right there, Hoss?" Mark looked at him, worry creased his brow.

"Sure," he replied, not having heard the question. "Hey, when was the last time you heard Greta sing?"

Mark shrugged. "Don't know. A while now. Can't honestly remember when."

Ben encouraged Greta into another song, and Trey wondered why she had stopped singing. Just like why had he stopped calling her 'magpie'? And why had they stopped making love? In his mind he heard her words from the night before, confirming how he hid from them all after Luke died. Every answer seemed to lead back to him.

The rolling in his stomach turned into an F5 tornado. Guilt weighed on him something fierce. How could he have let this happen? Had he really sucked all of the joy from Greta's life when he emotionally disappeared?

"Trey, honey, you're looking a little green. Are you sure

you're okay?" Greta knelt in the dirt before him.

"I'm not sure."

He had promised her a fresh start, no looking back, but the memory of how she had looked when she sang to their son had the tears burning in his throat. Why would he ever want to forget that?

Trey cupped his hand around the back of her neck. "I remembered you singing to Luke," he whispered in her ear.

Her body stilled. "You did?" Her hot breath brushed his cheek.

"Yeah, you rocked him when he was a little baby. And you sang. That was all. It was a wonderful memory."

She released a shaky breath and when she pulled back, tears filled her eyes. "That's good. I'm glad."

He brushed a soft kiss to her lips and then he held her tight. They stayed that way for a while as the party continued around them.

Chapter 13

"THAT WAS SUCH a great idea, Trey," Greta called out to him from the bathroom. "We should do that more often."

"Yeah, we should." He pulled back the bed covers. "Everyone seemed to enjoy themselves." He bit the inside of his thumb before taking the plunge. "Greta, why don't you sing anymore?"

She sauntered in, rubbing lotion into her hands. "What did you say?" She wore a short, lilac-colored silk nightgown. The sight of her long bare legs made him lose focus for a second.

Stay. On. Task. "Why don't you sing anymore?"

Her brow creased in amusement before she turned away with a shrug. "I don't know. It's not something I do with any regularity." She picked up a brush from the dresser and began to run it through her hair.

"You used to. You sang all the time. When you were happy, you sang."

She threw him a puzzled glance over her shoulder. "What makes you say that?"

"I remember. You'd sing or hum whenever you were happy."

"Really?" She licked her lip and shrugged. "I guess I never

paid attention."

"Why did you stop?" He knew he sounded like an old fish-wife, but he needed to know just how badly he had fucked up their relationship.

"I don't know." Her voice was sharp with annoyance. "Why do you keep asking me? It doesn't matter."

"It does to me." He caught her by the arm as she tried to pass by. "Don't you see? Steven and Adam have never heard you sing, and they're always buzzing around you. If you haven't been singing, then you haven't been happy. I know things fell apart with us, and it's my fault." His hands tightened on her shoulder. "I failed you. I made you a promise the day we met that I would never hurt you, and I failed." His voice broke.

"Oh, Trey, honey," Greta took his hands and placed a kiss in each palm before resting them against her heart. "You're making a mountain out of a mole hill. I know you've been through a lot lately, but whether or not I sing around the house is not important. The past is in the past. Last night was a new start. Remember?"

"I don't want to fail you again." Over the last few days, all he had seen were signs of his failures. The only success was the business. But the business couldn't hold him close or brush the hair out of his eyes. The business wasn't capable of love.

Her lips brushed his in a soft kiss. "All I need is you."

"But—"

"Do I make you happy?"

The question threw him. "Of course."

"How? When you think about it, you have known me for only a handful of days. I want you to think, *really* think. How have I made you happy?"

The word "everything" came to mind, but by her expression he knew she wanted a serious answer. "When you smile at me, I feel like I've been given something special. You listen to me and encourage me. You gave me a child and loved him with your whole heart. How can that not make me happy?"

Greta blinked back tears and slid her hands up his arms. Her heat thawed the icy frost that had encased him since his conversation with Jack.

"It's the same for me," she murmured against his lips. "I don't need you to be Superman. All I need is you. Just you."

An anxiety he didn't understand banded around his chest, squeezing his body until his heart felt ready to burst and his lungs burned. He needed to mark her, claim her, chain her to his side so that he would never lose her. He bent his knees to match her dainty height, his lips at the perfect level with hers to pour his fear and need into his kiss.

His fingers gripped the flesh of her ass, digging hard to hold her close, crushing the satin gown with the force of his hunger. Her arms clasped around his neck as she sagged in his hold.

"Greta," he gasped and buried his face into her neck when he broke for air. The pillars holding up his confidence crumbled and the ensuing collapse left him shaking.

"Shhh," she soothed. "I've got you, baby. I've got you. Let me show you what you mean to me."

She placed a tender kiss over his pounding heart before blazing a trail of biting kisses down his chest and over the hard muscles of his abs. She sank to her knees and traced a wet pattern around his navel with her tongue, before kissing every inch of lightly furred skin revealed as she unbuttoned his jeans.

The heavy stalk of his cock sprang free and fell right into her hands. Her palm swirled over the head once before she sucked the hard length into her mouth.

He groaned as his eyes crossed. The hot, moist, vacuum she created made his knees buckle. "Geez-us, woman. Are you trying to send me back to the hospital?"

The vixen peeked up at him from under lowered lashes. The corner of her lips curled into a wicked grin. His heart about gave out when her tongue flicked out to collect the pearly drop of cum that pooled on the tip. She wrapped one hand around the base while the other stroked and teased. Her nails raked across his abs, the muscles flexing under her touch. She trailed the tips over his hips and around to his ass as she swallowed his cock. She fingered the crease between his cheeks, reminding him of how she had touched him the night before and his shaft hardened to steel.

There she was on her knees, pleasing him like no woman had ever done before. Never had and never would again.

The desire to come threatened to take over all rational thought. As much as he loved to let go and feel her nimble tongue coax him to completion, he needed to immerse himself into her hot, willing body with a desperation bordering on insanity. He grabbed her under the arms and tossed her onto the bed. She barely had time to gasp before he was on her, tasting every inch of creamy skin he could get his mouth on. The strap of her gown broke in his haste to bare her luscious breasts. The moment the plump nipple beaded in the cool air, he suckled her like a man starved.

Her hiss of pleasure sent a jolt down his spine, making all of the little hairs on his body stand like antennae tuned to her response.

She hugged her silky thighs around his waist as she pulled him flush against her wriggling body. Her pussy was open and dripping with her honey as he positioned his cock at her entrance.

"Do you love me?" he asked in a harsh voice.

"What?" She blinked as if waking from a dream.

"Do you love me?"

"Yes." She brushed the hair from his forehead. The soft light in her eyes made him tremble. "Yes, I do."

"Tell me. Say it out loud," he demanded.

"I love you, Trey."

One plunge sent him deep into her core. The force of it had her arching her back as she cried out in shock.

"Again. Tell me again."

"I love you."

He thrust hard. "Again."

"I love you, I love you, I love you." The bite of her nails digging into the thick muscles of his back spurred him higher, further.

His rough palm caught on the delicate fabric of her gown as he held her hips in place. His other hand clenched the edge of the bed as he rode her hard. The need to get as deep inside her as physically possible overrode everything else.

Greta alternated between chanting his name and praising God as he made her take all of his driving length. Her hands smoothed over his shoulders, down her side and around to cup the curve of his butt, urging him to go faster.

"Trey," she choked out. Her body undulated beneath him as her sheath sucked on his cock.

"That's it, baby." He blinked against the sweat running into his eyes. "Take me. You're mine." A sizzling bolt of lightning streaked from his heart down to his balls. "Mine. Mine." The tip of his cock nudged her womb as fiery jets of cum shot out.

"Mine."

His spine bowed to keep as much of their bodies in contact as possible. Blackness stole his vision. Greta's scream echoed in his ears while she twisted and bucked beneath him. If he didn't remember his name before, he was pretty sure he would now.

He didn't know how much time had passed until his head finally cleared. "Greta?" Did that croaking voice belong to him?

"I'm here," she whispered.

In the low lamplight, he saw the silvery tracks of her tears. "Magpie, did I hurt you?"

"No." Aftershocks shook her body. "It's just never been that…intense before. It was like…" she trailed off with another shudder.

A possession. A claiming. Trey had marked her as his, forever.

Not able to part from her for one second, he curled around he and brushed his thumb over her damp cheek. "Greta?" He waited until she met his gaze. "I love you." He stopped the denial he saw coming. "I love you. From the moment I first saw you, I knew you were mine." He tasted the salt of her silent cry on his lips and tongue. "All I need is you, Greta. With you by my side, I can face anything."

And still she cried, whether from fear or happiness, he didn't know, but he needed her like he needed air. Like he needed sustenance. She made his world beautiful.

"I love you, Trey," she breathed out in a broken voice. "Always."

She burrowed her fingers in his hair and brought him down for a kiss. Her arms and legs clutched him close, encouraging him to smother her.

He thrust his cock, which had never softened, in and out of her sheath in a smooth rhythm that matched the beating of his heart. Limbs entwined, they clung to each other like moss on a stone, sinking into the essence of each other over and over again. Throughout the night Trey took her body until they collapsed where they lay. Even then he couldn't stop touching her, afraid that if he let go, she'd be lost to him forever.

Chapter 14

"WHATCHA DOING THERE, Trey?"

Ben's deep rumble made Trey jump in his seat. His ears burned as he glanced over his shoulder and saw Ben and Colby watching him with identical frowns on their faces.

He jumped down off the tractor he knew he shouldn't be on. "Baking cookies, what's it look like?" If you're caught doing something you shouldn't, then lash out with sarcasm. "I can't sit back while everyone else is working."

"Why aren't you in your office like usual?" Colby asked.

Trey hadn't been in that office since the moment he realized it had become his hiding place. The first chance he got, he was taking the computer and necessary files out of that cave and then boarding up the room. But not yet. The room gave him the creeps, and he wasn't eager to return.

"I thought the fresh air would do me some good." He reached for a bale of grass and held back the wince as the ligaments in his shoulder pulled tight.

"Well, there's getting fresh air and then there's hurting your-self. We'll give you a hand." Ben grabbed the nearest bale and easily hefted it onto the conveyor belt.

The hot sun beat down, and soon the sweat was rolling down his back and wetting his hair. But the work was good, honest, and sure beat being locked indoors all day.

From the corner of his eye, Trey watched both men as they worked. Colby was like a miniature version of Ben with similar brown hair and dark eyes, although Ben had a touch of gray at his temples.

At the age of twenty Ben had been hired by Trey's father. He was big then, but now the man was huge. He had seen Trey through all of his tough times. Now near the age of forty, he had no wife and no children that Trey had heard of, or could recall. It made him wonder why.

Besides Mark, Ben was the only ranch hand Trey remembered. He knew he had let Greta down in the past. Had it been the same with his men? They were men, so of course it wasn't like they would say, "Hey, Trey, I'm feeling unappreciated." But he remembered when there used to be fishing trips and football games and cookouts. When he locked himself away in that office, what did the hands think? Is that why most of them were gone now? And what had inspired the few who had stuck around to stay?

Questions, questions, and more questions. Soon he'd have enough of them baled and stacked to feed the entire herd during the winter.

The best course of action would be to say nothing and move forward. Only a pansy would instigate a Dr. Phil moment, yet he couldn't keep his trap shut. "Can I ask you guys something?"

Colby wiped the sweat from his brow with a handkerchief, then tucked it into his back pocket. "Shoot, boss."

"Why did you stay on when I was being a jackass?"

A cool, contemplative mask settled on Ben's chiseled features, while Colby looked at him like he just whipped out his johnson. He opened his mouth then snapped it closed and looked at Ben for guidance.

When Colby saw that the older man hadn't even blinked, he frowned and turned back to Trey. "What?"

Trey's lips twitched at the sight of the young man's confusion. Colby was probably trying to figure out an answer that wouldn't get him fired. "Why would you work for a man who treated you like a piece of farm equipment? Who never smiled, never asked after your welfare, who'd rather stay in a closet than spend time with those who cared about him?"

Colby's eyes widened. "You got your memory back."

His gut sank at the confirmation of his asshole status. "Not really." He nudged a bale with his boot. "I get the sense that I might have lost my way after Luke died. I don't think I was as personable as I once was."

"Well," Colby swallowed. "You weren't always like that. You just became distant." He let out a rough exhale and looked out into the horizon. His brow pinched as he scratched under arm near his armpit. "Look, I remember when Luke died. It was bad. I just figured that it was your way of grieving. You might have kept away, but you were always fair and willing to listen if any of us had an issue. Really, that's all I want in an employer. And as my friend, you had a really crappy thing happen to you. You needed time to heal."

Trey nodded, blinking against the cloud of dust that must have flown into his eyes. His gaze switched to Ben. So many emotions swirled in those dark, all-seeing eyes that Trey stood transfixed, hoping that the big man would deliver some sage words to help him come to terms with his action in the past.

Finally, Ben broke his gaze and ran a hand over his closely cropped hair. "Do you remember much about when your dad hired me?"

"Not really. I was twelve. One day I came downstairs and you were at the breakfast table."

A small smile touched his lips. "Your dad found me working, underage, at the Crescent Moon Bar. My father ran out on us when I was young, and my mom went through loser boyfriend after loser boyfriend until she left when I turned eighteen. Your dad offered me a home. Stability. A family. I've always thought of you, and Mark, and even Colby here—" he gave Colby a nudge with his elbow—"as my brothers. You're my family. I knew that one day you'd come back to us. It looks like you have."

Trey swallowed hard against the thump in his throat. As teenagers, Ben was the one who had watched out for him and Mark when they stole their first beers and dragged them home before their fathers found them missing. When he had had to bury his parents, it was Ben who guided him, encouraged him to keep the ranch, and work it himself. Had Trey always been blind to the support he had? He felt the moisture pooling in his eyes and nodded, too stunned to think of anything to say.

"Look, there's no need for you to do any heavy lifting, and I understand if you don't want to be cooped up. I know that if I was recuperating from an injury and I had a very pretty lady waiting to nurse me back to health, I wouldn't be out here in the manure. Colby and I will finish this. Why don't you go get Greta and take a drive somewhere?"

That sounded great, but he wanted to prove his worth. "Are you sure?"

"We got it, boss." Colby winked. "There's always something you can do around here later."

"Thanks." His voice came out hoarse. Trey cleared his throat and tried again. "Thank you."

The two men waved him away, and Trey left before he did

something stupid like bawl in front of them. It was quite humbling to realize just how much his family had been looked after. How much family he had and never realized. He was a lucky SOB to have these men working for him.

It didn't take much thought to plan out exactly how he wanted to spend his afternoon. Heat pooled in his groin at the thought of him, Greta, and an air mattress in the back of his truck. Man, he'd been waiting for an excuse to get the three of them together. Quality time with his wife was exactly what he needed.

GRETA SNIFFED AND adjusted her grip on the carving knife. She worked slowly, careful not to slice off a finger as tears blurred her vision. The onions sat off in the corner, waiting for their turn under the blade after she finished with the tomatoes.

Another tear slipped of her nose and splashed onto the blade to mingle with the juicy red fruit. At this rate, she was definitely going to draw blood. She set the knife down and curled over the counter. Gritting her teeth and clamping her jaw shut didn't keep the great sobs at bay as they tore out of her throat.

Trey's memory was returning and soon there would be no more pretending. Even if the possibility of all of his memory coming back was a ways off, the constant fear of discovery was driving her mad. Perhaps she should have told him the truth from the beginning. Maybe he would have been able to look at things from a different perspective and understand the situation. Oh, but now he looked at her like he used to, with that heat in his eyes that made her knees weak and want to throw herself into his arms. She had missed his kisses, the way he moved inside her body, the sound of his voice when he said he loved her. When she had begged to the heavens to have his love again, she hadn't known it was going to be at the cost of her sanity. Now her selfishness could leave her with nothing.

Would've, could've, should've. That train was long gone and there was no going back. The damage was done. The thought of never feeling his touch again made her tears flow faster and her entire body shake as they gathered on the counter under her cheek.

"Greta?"

She jumped at the sound of Mark's voice. Oh God, this was almost as bad as Trey finding her.

"What's wrong? Where's Trey?"

She wiped at her cheeks with a dishtowel and wished she had a mountain of chopped onions to explain the tears. "He's out in the field somewhere," she managed to get out between great gulps of air.

"Are you hurt? Did you cut yourself?"

She pressed her trembling lips together, and shook her head.

"Greta, you gotta talk to me. What's wrong?" He set his hat down on the countertop.

She took another watery breath and looked into his eyes, and another wave of helplessness crept over her head and swept her in the undertow. Over the years, Mark had become her best friend. Many nights, he sat with her on the swing and let her pour out her heart. Sometimes they said nothing, and his mere presence reminded her that she wasn't alone. She hated this weakness, this need to have a man hold her and tell her everything would be all right. She was a grown woman and capable of taking care of herself. But when he lowered his head and those dark eyes pierced right though her with a look that said to lay it on him and he'd see her through the sorrow, the need to bare all had become too great.

"I can't do this anymore," she admitted in a small, defeated voice. "I'm so afraid. I'm so tired of being afraid. He's going to remember, and it will be so bad." The tears started up again. "I can't, I just can't."

"Ah, Greta." Mark's posture deflated. With gentle hands under her elbows, he drew her into an embrace.

"No." She pushed away. "You shouldn't. I don't want—"

"Stop." He tucked the hair that stuck to her face behind her ear. "No matter what, I'm your friend. If I want to comfort you, then I'm gonna comfort you."

She put her head down and remained stiff in his arms as she tried to regain her composure.

He murmured soothing sounds while his hands traced up and down her back as he curled his bigger body around her. He rubbed his cheek against the top of her head, making strands of her hair catch in his stubble. The hug was friendly, but she knew that with just a word it could turn into so much more, which made her feel even worse.

The thought of running away with Mark had crossed her mind on more than one occasion. He never hid his feelings for her, and never pushed her for anything more than friendship. He was honest, respectful, and true to his word, not to mention that the man had a ripped body formed by years of physical labor and the face of a fallen angel. In her opinion, there was only one thing wrong with him.

He wasn't Trey.

Trey had owned her heart the moment she found him tossing pebbles at her window. It was his playfulness and determination she had fallen in love with. His confidence that together anything was possible had given her the freedom to believe in their love. No matter what lay in her future, her heart forever belonged to Trey. She knew that. Mark knew that too, yet there he stood, offering her comfort because she hurt and expected nothing in return.

It sickened her to think she might have been using his friendship to bolster her self-esteem. Mark deserved a woman of his own to love and who'd love him back just as fiercely. Falling apart in his arms wouldn't help him move on. If she was going to get her life back on track, she needed to stand on her own two feet. The future was a great, big unknown, with only one certainty. Herself.

She pulled away with a self-deprecating laugh. "You'd think I'd be all cried out by now."

"We all have our moments." He pinched her chin, drawing her gaze up. Concern darkened his eyes and drew the corners of his mouth down. "Everything will be fine, Greta. You just gotta have faith. And so what if he doesn't remember? He doesn't deserve you."

"Mark, stop." They've had this argument before. "Don't say that. He's been through a lot."

"So have you. I wish you wouldn't make excuses for him. Do you know how often I've wanted to hurt him for making you cry?" The roughness of his tone was in sharp contrast to the gentle hand he used to stroke her cheek.

"Please." She pulled away from the touch. "Please. Don't."

He looked out the window, a muscle ticking in his jaw as he ground his teeth together.

"All right," he said, meeting her gaze. "I'm sorry. I know he's trying. Sometimes, it's like the past few years haven't happened and he's his old self again. Don't fret about tomorrow, or the day after that. It's gonna work out. Somehow. You are a strong woman. You'll survive whatever is thrown at you."

"Yeah," she drew the word out. "I'll survive." Bitterness crept into her tone. She survived hard times before, but would she ever again be whole?

"Mark, I'm sorry." She shook the maudlin thoughts out of her head. "I didn't want to drag you into this or make things harder. You've been so good to me and I haven't... I wish, I wish..." she trailed off, her head hung low.

Mark reached out then drew his hand away to hook his thumb into his belt loop instead. "You've nothing to be sorry for. I make my own choices. I'm a big boy. I knew what would go down."

"You're a good man, Mark," she whispered, her eyes filling with more goddamn tears. She was going to be a prune by the end of the day if this kept up.

He inclined his head. His own lips were pressed together, as if he wanted to say something else, but thought better of it. He reached for his hat and twirled it in his hands. "I came to see how you were holding up. I guess I have my answer."

"I'm sorry." *For everything.*

He waved her apology away. "Do you need help with anything?" When she shook her head, he rapped his knuckles on the counter. "Don't hesitate to call me if you do."

"I will," she promised, as she vowed to never take advantage of him again.

She waited until the sound of his boots across the tile faded and the front door shut with a soft click before returning to work on the waiting vegetables. She rolled the big Walla Walla onion onto the cutting board and deftly sliced through the center. The sweet fumes rose up and stung her eyes, but she didn't shed a tear.

Chapter 15

TREY REELED AWAY from the sight of Mark staring at Greta as if he'd sweep her up into his arms and ride off into the sunset. He managed to stumble out the back door and sat with a hard bounce on the top step.

"Holy shit," he breathed out through lungs tight with shock.

His best friend was in love with his wife.

His brain exploded into a million pieces then rushed back to form one mind-numbing ball of mush.

His best friend was in love with his wife.

What the fuck?

How the hell had he missed *that?* It all made sense, though. Mark seemed to be rather familiar with her routine, her moods, her thoughts.

Shit, was this what Greta didn't want him to remember? Dear God, did she love Mark back? The thought made his stomach cramp and sent a sharp shooting pain over his right eye.

He climbed back to his feet on shaky limbs and searched the horizon for clarity. The pissed-off husband part of him wanted to storm in there and demand answers, while the chicken-shit part wanted to slink into the darkness of the barn and pretend he didn't know anything.

A crazed, tittering laugh escaped from his lips. He *didn't* know anything, that's why he felt like a kite twisting in the wind, ready to snap and sail into oblivion. Was it even possible to face either of them and pretend he hadn't been a witness to that exchange?

Hell no. One thing you learned while living on a ranch was that sooner or later you were gonna step in some shit. Chances were that if he kept quiet, he'd invariably end up ankle deep in a steaming pile of more lies. No matter how painful it might be, he needed to know exactly what was going on. The time for secrets was over, but first, he had questions for his best friend.

A peek through the glass revealed Greta alone in the kitchen, back at work cooking supper. Trey snuck past the window and rounded the side of the house.

Mark stood on the porch, staring into the distance in much the same way Trey had done just a moment before. Loss was etched into every line of his face and drew his shoulders down. He closed his eyes and let out a long, slow breath through his mouth. He slapped his hat against his thigh before jerking it onto his head and gliding down the stairs.

Trey ran after him, without a clue as to what to say. He reined in the furious emotions rioting inside him and tried to remain calm. This was going to require finesse and it wouldn't do to go off half cocked.

"You're in love with my wife," he shouted. Damn, that was smooth.

Mark froze mid-step as his shoulders formed a tense line. It seemed like an eternity passed before he turned around.

He raised his strong chin and looked Trey dead in the eye. "Yep."

Several seconds of silence slid by, and Trey felt like an ass as he waited for more. He knew better than to expect Mark to elaborate.

"Does she love you back?" Just asking the question burned his throat.

Mark's big shoulders slumped, but his dark gaze never wavered. "Greta has never treated me as anything other than a friend. She loves you."

The weight crushing Trey's chest eased enough to allow him to breathe. Relief filled him so fast, he became light headed. "Why was she crying?"

"I don't know," Mark ground out. "Why don't you ask her?"

"She won't tell me. She doesn't talk to me like she does you. Why won't she?"

Mark bit off a curse. "Maybe it's because *you* won't talk to her. Goddamn it," he snapped as his body trembled with restrained annoyance. "You know, I was okay losing her to you, because you treated her like she was the stars and moon combined. But when Luke died, we might as well have buried you next to him. You didn't just push everyone away. You either ignored us or treated us like we were nothing but property. Just more tools to keep the ranch running. And I had to stand by and watch a beautiful, passionate woman become a shell of herself under your coldness. If you want to fucking know what's wrong with your wife, go fucking ask her!" He pivoted on his dusty black boot and stalked away. He jerked a lighter out of his front jeans pocket and searched frantically through the rest of his clothes.

"Damn it!" he shouted when he came up empty, then threw the lighter into the field.

Four angry strides later he cursed again and jumped the fence. Retrieving his lighter from the dry grass, he jammed it back into his pocket then stomped back down the road.

As Trey watched him, his mind raced over the three things

he had just learned.

His best friend was in love with his wife.

Greta was still hiding something from him.

And he was never going to get his clean slate do-over.

The pressure to regain his memory landed on him like a two-ton bull. No way was he going to be able to move forward without understanding his past. He needed answers and he needed them now. Talking to Greta was out of the question. She was far too upset at the moment and might retreat if she thought he was pushing her.

He saw Mark disappear into the motor shed. Seconds later, the roar of a dirt bike tore through the quiet summer air before Mark shot out like a bat out of hell, disappearing into a grove of ponderosa pines.

Trey ached for his friend despite what just occurred. Greta was an easy woman to love, and Mark had met her first. That must have been a bitter pill to swallow, having her choose Trey over him. How difficult had it been to stand by and watch another man love her, and then toss her away? If Trey ever saw anyone mistreat her, they wouldn't be breathing for very long.

Was that how he got hurt? Had Mark finally become fed up with his behavior and tried to take him out? No, he instantly rejected that idea. Mark might be pissed at him, but he would never try to kill him. He hoped.

Damn, what a complete and utter fuckfest.

Trey turned back to the house, feeling older than ever. The windows of the upper story stared down at him like wise, all-knowing eyes. This was the house he was born in. It was where every event in his life happened. Happy or sad, ecstatic to downright devastating, the house had seen it all. He looked at the building, hoping that somehow all of the answers would spill out the front door.

An idea struck him like lightning. He sucked in a sharp breath and his heart began to pound so fast and so hard he thought he'd really been electrocuted.

There was one person who might be the key to unlocking his past.

He raced back to the house and tore up the stairs before he thought twice and pussed out. At the top of the landing he came to a screeching halt in front of the first door on the left. For five minutes, he stared at the white-painted wood, his hand on the doorknob, feeling more like an idiot with each passing second.

What was there to be afraid of? It was just him, the door, and the overwhelming urge to turn around and walk away.

"It's just a room," he scolded his shaking hand. "Get your head out of your ass and get inside."

He took a deep steadying breath, closed his eyes and twisted the knob with a jerk. Within seconds, he was inside the room, his back braced against the door. He waited for the rushing in his ears to fade and his pulse to slow before slowly opening his eyes.

A billowy soft maroon comforter covered the queen-sized bed. A dresser and a nightstand in a matching pale wood stain completed the furnishings in the sparsely decorated room. The only suggestion it had once been a nursery was the light blue paint on the walls.

Minutes passed as Trey waited for his memories to hit him over the head like a frying pan. When nothing happened, alarm began to set in. He was running out of options. This room was the key. He felt it in his gut. Luke had to be the answer to what was holding his memories back. There had to be something in the room to help him.

The closet door opened on silent hinges, exposing its secrets. The crib, disassembled and leaning against the back wall, had his heart racing. Besides the photo he found in his office, the crib was the only other item he'd seen that indicated a child had once lived there. Stacked on the closet floor were three unmarked boxes. Somehow Trey knew that was all that remained of Luke Armstrong.

"Please let this work. Please let this work," Trey whispered, half hopeful and half afraid it would. The way his hand now shook made the earlier trembling out in the hallway look steady enough to perform brain surgery.

A stuffed bear, a tiny football, and some very worn T-shirts lay inside the first box. Trey pulled a shirt out and smiled. On the white cotton was a silhouette of a cowboy, with tomato stains decorating the front. He held it up to his nose and inhaled. Laundry soap and clean baby skin. In his mind, he suddenly saw big, round, laughing blue eyes filled with mischief smiling up at him. Spaghetti stuck all over chubby cheeks and in his dark hair. Hysterical giggling preceded a well-aimed toss of more pasta on the wall.

The images that flooded Trey's mind brought him to his knees. He reached out a hand, his fingertips digging at the wall for support. He took in great gulps of air as it all came rushing back.

Luke.

He remembered Luke. The day he was born, just like Greta had described. The way he smelled, like baby lotion and sour milk. The light in his eyes when he caused trouble. It was all there.

And that horrible day when that light had gone out.

Trey had been out in the far pasture with Ben when Colby called his cell. Greta was screaming for help from Luke's bedroom. The three of them jumped on their dirt bikes and raced back to the house. The sound of their bikes had been drowned out by the roaring blades of the medivac as it touched down in the huge driveway.

He hadn't even brought the bike to a complete stop before he leaped off and ran into the house and up the stairs. The panic that gripped him made him stumble several times along the way. His heart had beat so hard, his eyeballs throbbed.

Greta's cries echoed down the hall. She had never made that sound before. It looped around his throat and strangled him with terror. The door stood opened, but momentum had him bursting into the room. He froze in the face of the nightmare that waited.

Luke was laid out in the floor, and Greta was holding his hand. Deep wrenching grief poured from her despite her efforts to hold it together and remain calm. Mark was bent over, performing CPR on the limp little body on the carpet.

Shock held him immobile as all of the color leeched from his vision. This wasn't supposed to happen. He was only two, for Christ's sake. What the hell happened? The paramedics shoved him out of the way as they entered. He bounced off the wall and would have fallen if Ben hadn't been there to catch him. Mark scrambled out of their way, but Greta held on. She refused to let go for one second.

It had been too late. Luke was gone and there was nothing Trey could have done to save him.

As he huddled in the closet, all of the pain, anger and help-lessness he felt that day resurfaced. Blood filled his mouth as he bit his lip to keep the sobs inside. Tears fell like rain to wet the shirt still clutched in his hands.

This was why he had pushed everyone away. This burning, tortuous ache of loss and failure that covered him like a dark, suffocating blanket.

He had been terrified that everyone else he loved would die, too. His mom, dad, Luke, even his former horse had all been taken too early. And Greta. If Greta was taken from him, he wouldn't be able to go on. That was why he stopped touching her. What if they had another child who suffered Luke's fate or, God forbid, Greta died in childbirth? The possibilities ate at him until he went mad with the constant worrying. He stopped sleeping, stopped eating. The paranoia had grown and grown until it had become too much to bear. He didn't want to hurt anymore. He didn't want to feel. So he stopped.

He stopped feeling.

No more taking meals with the rest of the family. The office was moved into the barn to stay away from the temptation of being near Greta. A fence went up around his heart. He could see out, but nothing and no one was allowed in.

Greta had been so hurt and confused by his withdrawal. She gave him time to grieve, but there was only so much distance she allowed. She tried to talk to him, yelled at him, cajoled him. She even asked him to seek counseling, but he kept avoiding her. Finally, she had given up. They coexisted in the same house, with no love, no sharing, but he knew she was safe. He had thought that the arrangement was going well until the day she left him.

Holy shit. He fell back on his ass as he remembered the day of his injury.

"She left me."

Chapter 16

THE DAY HAD begun the same as the last four hundred and eighty-two. It was four in the morning and the dawn was hours away, leaving Trey in the near dark of the empty kitchen.

He scraped the last of the bran flakes out of his bowl before placing it in the dishwasher. The light above the stove illuminated the ingredients Greta had left out on the counter. It looked as though she was planning on making waffles for the men that morning. Trey's stomach grumbled in protest at having been subjected to mushy cereal. He didn't blame it. Greta's waffles were the best.

His sigh of longing came out of nowhere and surprised him. Sure, he hadn't shared a meal with anyone in a long while, but that was how he wanted it. Mealtime was when most of the talking occurred. When everyone shared parts of their day or interesting things they learned. It was a time to bond, and he didn't want to bond with anyone any more than he had to.

No, he thought as he turned off the light, plunging the room into darkness. It was better this way.

The office was exactly as he had left it the night before. His weights were where he set them, and the book he had finished rested on top of the others he had read that week. Of course, he hadn't expected any different. Mark was the only one who ventured in from time to time, mostly to check if Trey was still breathing. Otherwise, he was left alone.

Only an hour had passed when he found himself staring at the ceiling and tapping his foot in agitation. Bills were paid. All of the reports were updated. He already read all of the books stacked around him. The men had been given their assignments for the day the night before. Unless he wanted to join them, there was nothing left for him to do in his office. The thought of taking another online computer course or playing a video game made him want to go back to bed. His lonely bed. Hell, he could probably take apart his computer and put it back together in a few hours if he really wanted to. But he didn't want to. He wasn't meant to be chained to a desk. He was supposed to be outside, working the land, watching over the livestock. It was still early and probably safe to go out in the field without running into anyone.

Sunlight had barely edged over the horizon by the time he saddled up Lucky in the barn. Pink and yellow fingers of light fought to break in through the cracks in the wood. Usually, they used dirt bikes to cover large areas, but Trey wanted to take his time. Plus, it had been a few weeks since he'd taken Lucky out. The exercise would do them both good.

A breeze stirred up, blowing the grass into an ocean of rolling green waves. Every blade was trimmed to his specifications, and only a few sections of fence needed mending. All in all, the ranch was in perfect condition. Trey surveyed his small kingdom with pride. He poured all of his sweat and time into the land. There was not one inch he hadn't explored and analyzed to get the most out of the resources. The land was all he had.

The land was all he had.

What would happen once he was too old to take care of the ranch? What would happen to him? There were people he trusted, like Mark and Ben, who could take over without any difficulty. Maybe one of them would have a child they could pass it on to. But where would that leave Trey?

This self-imposed exile was becoming impossible to maintain. Especially when he saw the strain it put on Greta. He hadn't spoken more than a word or two to her in weeks, and she had begun sleeping in her workroom. She no longer gifted him with her smiles, not that he did anything to earn them. In fact, the whole crew had long ago stopped trying to engage him in any conversation that wasn't absolutely necessary. They learned he was no longer the carefree, fun-loving man he once was. That Trey was long gone, swallowed up by the pain of loss. Caring hurt too damn much.

God, he felt old. Was this what isolation did to you? Made your bones ache and your head hurt? Made your lungs feel like lead weights and your blood sluggish as it tried to keep the heart that you no longer acknowledged you had pumping?

Birds chirped in the trees and the bright sunshine mocked the mental darkness he resided in. He couldn't stay cooped up all of the time, yet the cheer of the outdoors reminded him of all that he rejected. How much longer could he keep this up?

It was after two in the afternoon when he returned to the barn. Eight more hours to occupy himself until he could go to sleep and another day would be over.

Out in the driveway, the open tailgate of the SUV and the sight of Greta loading boxes into the back caught his attention. Frowning, Trey wondered what she was doing. Didn't she attend an art fair last week? He hated it when she left. He worried about her safety when she was off the ranch, and he hated the fact that he still worried. Greta was capable of taking care of herself. But what if she found herself in a situation that was out of her control and he wasn't there to help her?

If he failed...

It would kill him, if he failed her like he had Luke.

Greta slid a suitcase into the backseat, filling the car to bursting. None of the hands were around, which really had Trey wondering what she was up to. Usually, one of the men went with her to help set up her booth.

His curiosity got the better of him and he strolled across the gravel. "Going somewhere?" he asked as he came up behind her.

Greta jumped and turned toward him with pale cheeks and startled eyes. "I thought you were out riding. I didn't see Lucky in the barn." Her voice held a shaky tremor, and her gaze darted everywhere but at him.

"I'm done. Where are you going?" Even as he asked, a rolling sensation began in his stomach. Something was wrong.

A mask of nothingness settled over her once-loving and glowing features. It was a look he knew well, since he felt it on his own face every day. She didn't want to tell him. This breakdown in communication was one he cultivated. The cool contempt in her eyes, when once she looked at him as if he were her sun, was his creation. Seeing what his coldness had done to her cracked a little of the shield he had built around his heart.

"I'm going to Seattle. There's an art show."

The news eased a bit of his tension. "Oh. When are you coming back?"

She blinked at him once, then twice. "I'm not coming back."

His brain knew the words, but he didn't comprehend. "What?"

"I'm not coming back," she stated, as if that was the end of the discussion. She closed the hatch then moved toward the driver's door.

"Wait, wait. Just wait." He blocked her way. The blood pounded in his ears and his lungs struggled for air. This was not part of the plan. She was supposed to stay here where she would be safe. "You're just leaving? Like that? Without even telling me?"

Her eyes widened, and that spark of fire within her that hadn't completely died flared. "You left over a year ago. I'm just making it official." She dodged to the left.

"Stop, just stop." His hands shook as he lifted his hat to wipe the sweat off of his brow with his sleeve. She was right, he had checked out, but the thought of her leaving made panic claw at his chest with rusty fingernails. "I know I've been distant, but I needed," he swallowed hard, "I don't—I can't—". Damn it, didn't she know? Didn't she understand?

"He was my son, too." Her low tone was a mixture of compassion and contempt. "Don't you think I hurt? That I don't miss him every day? But I'm grateful for every second he was mine. I want to talk about him, remember him. You want to pretend that he never existed. I'm not going to hide in a hole and wait to die. I want to live. I want love. I want a partner who will always be there, no matter what. I deserve better." She stood there, shoulders back, chin up, so proud. The strength that flowed from her was so much more than he was capable of. He both envied it and cursed it.

"Greta, please." His throat burned as he felt her slipping away. He was supposed to lose her when he died of old age, not because she walked away. "I'll try. I promise. Just give me a chance."

"No. You can stay here and rot, if that's what you want, but I'm not going to rot with you. I'm done."

"Please!" he barked. All of the emotions he bottled up for the past year started to boil. He had to stay calm and settle this rationally. "Let's go inside and talk this out." If he just got her inside, he could convince her to see his side.

"No. Don't touch me." She brushed away his outstretched hand. "It's over, Trey. I'm done talking and I'm done waiting."

"Greta, please," he tried again. She had to stay. He latched on to her arm.

"Don't touch me!" she screamed and shoved him in the chest with so much force, he stumbled back a few steps.

Now it was serious. Greta had never physically struck out at him before. She was an expert at putting someone in place with her words, but she had never laid a hand on anyone. Without a single clue as to how to respond, he stood there and stared at her.

Taking advantage of his stunned silence, she jumped into the car. Her face contorted as she tried to hold back her tears. Gravel sprayed all over as she tore out of the driveway, barely missing him by inches.

He didn't know how long he had stood there staring in the direction of her taillights. The dust from the tires had long since settled by the time he remembered to blink. The sun had started to set over the hillside, and the temperature dropped and a chill settled in his bones, but the cold he felt in his heart was not due to the weather.

Numb to the world, he began to walk. One heavy plodded footstep after the other, he kept moving. Not seeing, not feeling, he hadn't even realized he had climbed back onto Lucky until they were a few miles away from the house.

As if sensing his shock, the world froze around him. The air was still, not a bee buzzed past him. Even the sound of the horse's hooves was absorbed by the hard earth.

Be careful what you wish for, they say. Wasn't this what he wanted, to be left alone? Two smoldering embers sat behind his eyes. A fiery hand gripped his heart and he doubled over the horn of the saddle. It wasn't supposed to hurt this bad. He had closed himself off so that when he lost her to death, it wouldn't hurt. This pain was a thousand times worse because he lost her to his own stupidity.

No longer able to control his stomach, he bent over and gulped in a great big lungful of air. Only the reins looped around his hand kept him from tumbling off the saddle. His head felt like a lead balloon and his entire body went from icy shivers to sweaty hot flashes.

God, he was such a fool. Greta was only going to live in the shadows for so long. Who would want to stay married to someone who treated you like the center of their world one minute then like you didn't exist the next?

Under the horse's hooves, the landscape changed from lush grass to a field of wildflowers. Lucky led them right to the huge elm tree by the stream. Their elm tree. The place where Luke was conceived. Trey had always felt safe and loved under the leafy branches. His stomach lurched again at the thought of Greta never holding him again on a warm summer night under the stars.

This couldn't be it for them. What, she leaves and he'd never see her again? Never hear her sing? Despite holding his wife at arm's length, he was always aware of where she was and what she was doing. He never stopped loving her. He was just afraid of the cost he paid for loving her.

The knowledge that she was going to start a new life, love someone else, was unacceptable. *He* wanted her. *He* wanted to bask in her light. *He* wanted to make her smile.

He was tired of being alone.

Trey straightened in the saddle. This was not the end. She still cared for him, otherwise she wouldn't have been so upset when she left. There had to be a way to convince her he was going to change. Not knowing where she went would slow him down, but he wasn't going to let that deter him. He'd make some phone calls and hunt her down.

Nothing else mattered but getting her back.

TREY BLINKED AS Luke's tiny shirt came into focus. His memory of everything after deciding to go after Greta was gone. Nothing but blackness and shadows. Perhaps he would never know how he became injured, but now he understood the truth about his marriage.

After smoothing out the creases in Luke's shirt, he placed it back in the box with the others. His own shirt sleeve made an impromptu handkerchief as he wiped at his wet cheeks. For a guy who prided himself on being a tough guy, he was sure doing a lot of blubbering lately. But these were good tears. He had his answers now, and he knew what he had to do to go forward. It was time to confront Greta and make her come clean.

Chapter 17

"YOU LEFT ME." Trey's voice cracked like a whip in the silent kitchen. His raw throat made his statement sound harsher then he intended. Maybe he should have started with "Hello."

The pen in Greta's hand went skidding across the paper. Her entire body appeared to freeze where she stood at the counter before her head whipped around so fast, the ends of her hair slapped her face. "What?"

"The day I got hurt. You left me."

The beautiful blush drained from her cheeks. She sagged against the counter. "You remembered." It wasn't a question.

"Yeah, I remembered. Everything." He took a step closer. His arms hung loose by his side in case she bolted and he had to give chase. "I remember Luke, and the day you left."

She didn't move. She didn't even look as though she was breathing. Wariness and fear darkened her eyes and turned the knuckles of her hands white where they gripped the edge of the counter.

"How did you find out I was hurt?" he asked.

"Mark called me."

The mention of Mark made his eye twitch, but he stayed on

task. "Why did you come back?"

The muscles of her throat worked as she swallowed. "You were hurt," her sweet voice rasped. "They didn't know what happened. When Mark called, he said that you were found bleeding and that it was bad."

"So guilt brought you back?"

"Yes. No." She closed her eyes, shaking her head. Her breathing began to escalate and her hands flitted from her throat to her hair then back to the counter. "I didn't want you hurt. I never wanted you hurt. The longer you were unconscious, the more scared I was that you wouldn't wake up, but then I was afraid that if you did—" she broke off and spun away. She sucked in big gulps of air as she fought back tears.

"Don't." He stepped behind her, trapping her in his arms. "Don't hide. Tell me, good or bad."

A small whimper escaped. "I was afraid you were going to wake up, and it was going to be the same. Part of me wanted you to stay asleep forever." Self-hatred glistened in the eyes she turned on him. "How horrible is that? I love you so much, but I hate what you became. I'd rather you died than wake up and have things the way they were. What kind of person does that make me that I wanted you dead?"

"Baby doll," he moaned when the first teardrop slid down her cheek. He pulled her stiff body against him. She hunched into a ball and he bet she would have disappeared into the floor if he'd let her. "Please don't feel bad. You were right," he murmured into her hair. "You were right about everything. Losing Luke hurt so badly, and if I lost you, I knew I wouldn't survive. And I didn't." He placed his hands on either side of her face, resting his forehead against hers. "I don't want to live without you, Greta. Losing you like that was the most painful thing I ever felt, because it was my fault. I stopped living, but without you… God, Greta, you're my world."

"I don't want to be your world." She blinked up at him with shimmering eyes and curled her fingers around his wrists. "I just want to share it with you."

This was why he loved her. She never sought to change him, who he really was. She only wanted to share experiences, to build, grow, and learn with him.

"I love you. I know I don't deserve you," he whispered against her lips. "But I'm not letting you go. Not again. I need you."

She took a deep breath through her nose and tightened her lips to keep them from trembling. His Greta, always so strong.

"I love you, Trey." She pressed a kiss to the corner of his lips.

"Thank you." It was an inadequate response, but it was the best he could think of at the moment. He had used up all of the flowery words and sentiments he knew.

Well, there was one other way he knew of to convey his love and need.

He tried to keep his kiss gentle, but the relief that everything was going to be all right drove the tumultuous river of his emotions over the banks. For a man who tried to remain in control of his feelings, the day had been a tornado that left him raw.

Her downy-soft lips parted, letting him give and take as he pleased. He felt the trust she placed in him like a physical caress on his soul. "Lord, woman, you drive me insane. Please, don't leave me."

"I won't. Not unless you go away again." She brushed the hair off his forehead. Her eyes squinted with menace even as her lips quirked up at the corner.

"I promise." He chuckled as he trailed kisses down her neck.

Her vanilla and jasmine scent intoxicated him. It soothed his weary heart and made his blood race at the same time. The cotton work shirt and jeans he wore suddenly felt rough and scratchy. Like a sponge, he needed to soak up her heat and love. Needed her velvety soft skin against him.

"Trey," she gasped when he had her shirt over her head a second later. "What are you doing?"

"I'm claiming my woman," he stated between kisses. "Right here, right now,"

Thank the lord for snaps, he thought as he stripped his shirt off while walking her back toward the table.

She fought his hands as he pulled at her jeans. "Trey, not here. Someone could walk in." She hissed when her bare butt hit the table's cold surface.

"This from the woman who surprised me in the horse barn one afternoon wearing nothing but a smile?"

"You remember that?" She was so cute when she blushed.

"Oh yeah, magpie. Every sigh, every moan. The way you screamed so loud, you actually caused a stampede." His fingers found her wet and open. She could protest all she wanted, but her body was ready and eager for him.

"It was only six cows," she panted, trying to keep her hips still.

"We should try it during mating season. Give them some inspiration."

Her pink tongue flicked out to wet her lips when he freed his cock. He pushed his jeans down just enough to give him some room. When she took him firmly in hand, his eyes rolled to the back of his head. There was his wildcat. In a few firm strokes, cum beaded at the tip and his balls drew up tight. No way he was going to last.

He pushed her back onto the table and stepped between her

spread thighs. "That's it, baby doll. Guide me home."

He loved the way she held her breath as he pushed his cock in deep. Her nails scored his back then dug into his glutes. "Please. Hurry."

"This time," he agreed with long hard strokes. "But later, I'm gonna love you any way and every way."

"Promise?" There was a little too much sass in her voice for his liking. Trey was ready to weep at the pleasure gripping him, and he needed her to beg for the same relief.

"Oh yeah," he promised. Then he set a hurried pace that had the heavy table rocking on its legs in a frantic rhythm.

The love in her eyes would have brought him to his knees if he hadn't been half lying down already. She was here, in his arms, and he was inside her. Not just physically, she carried him in her heart, just like she was in his soul.

The elation he felt brought him to the edge, fast and hard. Thankfully, she was right there with him. Her pussy squeezed him tight, little ripples promising paradise. "Come on, baby doll. Come with me."

When it hit, the release nearly blew his head off and had spots dancing in front of his eyes. Greta writhed beneath him, trapped by his hips. Blood tinged her mouth from where she bit her lip to keep her screams in. Tears leaked from her eyes as her compact body milked him for every drop he produced.

His arms gave out the same time her legs fell from his waist. Exhaustion the likes of which he had never felt before swamped him and dragged him under. After such an intense, roller coaster of a day, his mind was ready to shut down.

"Holy shit," Greta breathed out in a shaky voice.

Trey lifted his head in surprise at her language. His laughter started with a few chuckles, then gained in momentum when she joined in. He was so sated that he fell to the floor when she pushed him off her.

"It feels so good to laugh." She pushed a tangle of hair off her wet cheeks as she sat up.

"Yeah." He nodded and tried to sit up. Nope. Not happening. He lifted his head off the tile and met her gaze. "We'll be doing more of that, too."

The smile she gifted him with told him she understood. They really were going to be all right. The weight that lifted off his shoulders made him feel like he was suspended in zero gravity.

While he floated in a warm, fuzzy cloud of satisfaction, Greta slid off the table and reached for her jeans.

"Why are you covering up?" He frowned.

"I'm not giving the guys a free show. Unless…" She smoothed her hands over her plump breasts as she straightened her T-shirt.

He was on his feet in an instant. "No way, magpie. I don't want to give Steven any ideas."

The sound of the back door closing followed by heavy footsteps had Trey rushing to tuck his shirttails in. Mark paused in the doorway with his hat in his hands.

Trey silently cursed as Mark's eyes darkened. He could only imagine what the two of them looked like, and by the tightening of his friend's features, he had a pretty good idea. The last thing he wanted to do was throw this in the face of his best friend.

"I take it you two are all right now?" Mark spun the hat between his palms with a nervous energy.

"We're going to be fine," Trey answered. "I got my memory back."

A dark eyebrow hitched up at that. "All of it?"

"Pretty much."

"Well, that's – that's good." His shuffling feet made Trey anxious. "That makes what I'm going to say easier then."

Trey's gut clenched. Mark was hurting, and there was nothing Trey could do to help. And Mark knew that too, which made the entire situation extra shitty. If Trey knew his friend at all, Mark wasn't going to wallow in self-pity. Which begged to question what was Mark thinking behind his dark eyes.

"I'm leaving."

Greta's breath hitched as if she'd been stabbed. Trey placed a comforting arm around her shoulders.

"Where are you going?" he asked, understanding why Mark needed some time away, but damn it, he didn't want his friend to go.

"Don't know yet. I think I'll see my mom for a bit."

"When are you leaving?"

"Tomorrow."

"For how long?" Greta asked.

His gaze landed on the tiles at his feet. "I may not come back."

"No!" "Why?" Trey and Greta shouted at the same time.

"Look," Trey started again in a more reasonable tone. "Greta, Mark has some things he needs to take care of, and now that I'm back on my feet, he can take care of them." He turned back to Mark. "Go do what you have to do. Just remember that you always have a home here. You're family. Always." He blinked his eyelids faster as Mark's image began to waver.

"I don't understand." Greta brushed away a tear on her cheek, which seemed to break Mark's cool, unflappable resolve.

"Come here, Greta girl." He opened his arms.

She flew to him and hugged him tight. "Are you leaving because of me?" Trey heard her ask in a quiet voice.

"No, don't think that." Mark ran his hand over her hair. "I need to go off and have a few adventures of my own. Take care of my boy." He said the words to Greta, but his gaze burned into Trey's. "Don't let him get too soft. And if he falls out of line, kick his ass."

She tried to smile but failed. "Okay." She brushed the hair off his forehead. "Be safe. And don't leave without saying good-bye. I'll pack you a sandwich."

"I won't," he said. Trey knew he would be gone long before the sun came up. "Well, I better get to packing."

Trey held out his hand. When Mark took it, Trey pulled him into a hug. They exchanged a few well-placed slaps on the back that said more than any words could've expressed. "Take it easy, Little Joe."

Mark's lips twitched slightly, but his eyes glowed with un-spoken emotion. "Thanks, Hoss."

Trey hugged Greta tight after Mark left with one last bitter-sweet smile. "He's in love with you. He told me."

Tears welled in her eyes. "I never meant for that to happen."

He placed a finger on her lips when she would have contin-ued. "I know that. And Mark knows that. I guess he needs to step back and figure out what it is that he needs to move on with his life. It couldn't have been easy on him. Especially with the way I've been acting. If it was me, I would have taken me out a long time ago."

"We're never going to see him again, are we?" She stared at the empty doorway, and Trey realized she had just lost her closest friend. Mark had been there for here when he was not. The separation was going to be tough on everyone, and Trey was prepared to make it as painless for her as possible.

"He'll be back." He placed a kiss to the top of her head. "This land is as much his as it is mine. It'll call him back."

"I hope so. I just want him to be happy. Wherever he is. Like us."

Trey curled her tighter into his embrace and buried his face in her neck. It felt so good to finally be on solid ground with her. "Are you really happy, Greta?"

A touch of wickedness edged her giggle. "Oh yeah. As long

as you don't go and do something stupid."

A pinch to the backside made her yelp. "I make no promises about not doing stupid shit, but I promise no more hiding."

"Me too." She kissed him on the lips to seal her promise.

"Would it be stupid if we went out for a little ride right now?" he coaxed, using his most persuasive tone.

"That sounds nice, but I have to get dinner ready."

"Magpie, these are grown men who all have their own kitchens in their quarters. Come on." If he had to get on his knees and beg, he would. "I've been wanting to get you in the back of my truck something fierce."

She worried her lip, making it puffy and kissable. While he was distracted, she plucked the keys from his belt with lightning-quick reflexes and ran down the hall. "I drive!" she shouted.

"Like hell," he roared.

Greta was halfway across the driveway before he caught her around the waist and tossed her over his shoulder. The little she-devil worked her hand between his skin and his jeans to pinch him in delicate places.

"Stop it, woman, or I'll drop you on your head." He punctuated the threat with a tap on the butt that made her giggle.

He dumped her in the cab with a scowl that quickly melted in the face of the pure love and joy that radiated on her face as she smiled up at him. He couldn't wait to show her again just how much he loved her.

After jumping in on his side, he pressed a firm kiss to her willing lips, thanking his lucky stars to be given a second chance.

"Buckle in, baby doll. I'm about to give you the ride of your life," he warned before tearing off down the road, leaving nothing but laughter and dust behind them.

ABOUT ANNA ALEXANDER

Anna Alexander's literary world changed at age thirteen when a friend gave her Kathleen E. Woodiwiss' *A Rose in Winter*. With her mind thoroughly blown, Anna decided that one day she too would become a romance novelist. With Hugh Jackman's abs and Christopher Reeve's blue eyes as inspiration, she loves spinning tales about superheroes finding love.

The Cloudy skies over her Pacific Northwest home give her plenty of opportunity to indulge in her passions, which are reading, writing and snuggling with a steaming cup of Irish coffee. Now if she could only find a hot Irishman to go with it, then life would be perfect.

Anna welcomes comments from readers.

Website
http://annaalexander.net/

Facebook
https://www.facebook.com/pages/Anna-Alexander/282170065189471?ref=hl

Twitter
https://twitter.com/AnnaWriter

Newsletter
http://eepurl.com/Q0tsz

ALSO BY ANNA ALEXANDER

Men of the Sprawling A Ranch Series

The Cowboy Way

The Marlboro Man – Spring 2015

Heroes of Saturn Series

Hero Revealed

Hero Unleashed

Hero Unmasked

Hero Rising

Cavern Series

A Night at The Cavern

Only at The Cavern – Winter 2014

Printed in Great Britain
by Amazon.co.uk, Ltd.,
Marston Gate.